A Letter
for Julie

OTHER WORKS BY THIS AUTHOR

THE LUCY TRILOGY

Call Mama
Scamper's Find
The Leci Legacy

Before Lucy: prologue to The Lucy Trilogy

SHORT STORY COMPILATION

A Tale or Two and a Few More

FOR CHILDREN

The Clock That Lost Its Tick and Other Tales

NOVELLAS

A Case for Julie
A Break for Julie
A Letter for Julie

A STAND ALONE NOVEL

Our Nipper

A Letter for Julie

TERRY H. WATSON

RamoanPress

Published in 2020 by Ramoan Press

ISBN Paperback: 978-1-9996502-8-5
Ebook: 978-1-9996502-9-2

A CIP catalogue copy of this book can be found in the British Library.

Published with the help of Indie Authors World
www.indieauthorsworld.com

IndieAuthors
World

DEDICATED TO

Drew, my husband and soulmate, on the occasion of his eightieth birthday.

The youngest, gregarious octogenarian I've ever come across.

Love you forever.

IN PRAISE OF THE JULIE SINCLAIR INVESTIGATES NOVELLAS

'An enjoyable read. So inventive, accurate, and realistic. Another well-written book from this talented author.
Christine Tait

'I love the way in which the author re-connects the reader to points from the previous book, so that nothing is missed.'
M.J. Martin

'Readers of the Lucy Trilogy will love the Julie Sinclair Investigates novella series.' *E.M. Archondakis*

'This novella series is part Murder She Wrote with just a pinch of a thriller thrown in, and all stirred up with the exceptionally unique voice of this author.'
Rebecca Forster, USA Today & Amazon bestselling author

ACKNOWLEDGEMENTS

As always, my thanks to you my readers who, by your positive comments and reviews, have encouraged me to continue writing.

Thanks, too, to my first proofreaders, Drew Watson and Emma Archondakis, and Donegal Sue for the craic.

To Christine McPherson for professional editing, and finally to Kim and Sinclair Macleod at Indie Authors World for assistance with publication.

A Letter for Julie

'Caroline, Caroline. Wait. Stop. Please, Caroline.'

The voice became louder, more irritating the nearer it got to the four ladies who were walking four abreast, having left the theatre after an entertaining show. Julie Sinclair and her two best friends from schooldays, Liz and Maggie, were accompanied by Maggie's daughter, Letitia – all four in jovial mood as they headed towards the centre of Edinburgh. As the theatre emptied, it appeared that the full capacity of theatre-goers, around three thousand, spilled out onto the street like a herd of noisy, raucous football fans whose team had just won a match.

The four linked arms, chatted non-stop about the performance, and tried to keep together while the crowds surged forward intent on reaching the various clubs and bars that were ready to welcome their patronage.

It was summer in Edinburgh, and the capital was alive with Festival fever. For once, the fickle Scottish weather was favourable, bringing a plethora of visitors to the city. It was still light; the sun had yet to set as the revellers filled the city with good - humoured banter.

Maggie remarked, 'I can't get used to it being light at this time of night. When I was a child living on the island, I was used to the simmer dim but since I've lived down south, I've

11

forgotten that five hundred miles makes such a difference.' She linked arms with her daughter and smiled as she looked at the face of her adult child.

'That was the best performance ever,' remarked Letitia, as she held the mother's arm in a closeness that emphasised the close bond between them. The two rarely saw each other, so relished time together.

'It certainly was, darling. A good belly laugh blows the cobwebs away. I don't know when I last laughed as much.'

As the crowd neared Princes Street, some revellers veered off into York Place, past the metropolitan cathedral to the various street beyond, to reach their destination.

'Let's head to Princes Street Gardens and have a last look at the Festival stalls before we return to the hotel,' suggested Liz. 'It's such a lovely evening, I want to make the most of it.'

This was to be their last evening together before Letitia returned to her job as a researcher into cancer cells – a job that had seen her honoured for her past research. She rarely took time off, but had been persuaded to do so by her father, the Rt. Hon. Jonathan Andrew Sinclair Smythe -Watkins, known to all as Jonny.

'Letitia, darling, I'm concerned that you never take a break from your demanding job. You know what they say about all work and no play,' he'd advised, when they'd spoken on the telephone. 'Please give some thought to join-ing your mother at Festival time in Edinburgh. She misses you dreadfully, and you would enjoy meeting up again with Julie and Liz.'

'I expect you are right, Dad, as always,' she'd laughed, as she pictured her father's serious face. 'I'll give it some thought.' And, to the delight of the others, she had joined them for the three-day break.

Now, as they walked through the busy streets of Edinburgh together, a voice seemed to follow them, becoming louder.

'Caroline. Please stop. We have to talk. Don't ignore me.'

Julie whispered, 'I wish Caroline, whoever she is, would stop before that guy blows a fuse. He seems really stressed.'

As they walked on, the voice came closer. Julie, walking on the outside of the group, could almost feel his breath on her neck.

The male owner of the voice finally caught up with the four, passed on Julie's right, then turned, and with his face level with hers, shouted, 'Caroline, for goodness sake. Stop. We need to talk.'

Julie, looking bemused, stared at the stranger and said, 'Please, go away. You are in my space.'

Dejected, the man shook his head, and before vanishing among the mass of people, turned towards the women in defiance.

'We can't go on like this,' he said. 'We need to talk. Your friends can't shield you forever.'

'What on earth was that about?' asked Julie of her companions. 'Who was that guy, and who the heck is Caroline?'

'Hey, Julie,' remarked Liz with a twinkle in her eye, 'do you have a secret admirer? Tell all.'

They all laughed at Liz's attempt to defuse the disturbing encounter.

The incident was forgotten as the friends crossed North Bridge, past the luxurious Balmoral Hotel and Waverley railway station, where they waited patiently for the traffic to ease. Once in the gardens, they wandered along past the iconic gothic Scott Monument where tourists, in various distorted poses, attempted to capture the two-hundred-foot structure on cameras and iPads.

'One of my literary heroes,' explained Julie, as she stretched her neck to view the top of the structure. 'Sir Walter Scott is an inspiration for writers, and the view from the top of his monument on a clear day is spectacular.'

As Liz looked up to view the top of the structure, she staggered and would have fallen had Maggie not caught her by the arm.

'Steady on, girl. You'll make us all dizzy. Who's for some mulled wine?' she asked, looking towards a nearby stall where revellers stood around drinking the warm nectar. 'It's years since I've had mulled wine.'

'It's something I associate with winter and Christmas, but let's have some to take the chill off,' Julie replied. Being the tallest, she caught the attention of the server and ordered their drinks.

An easterly wind caused a chill from the river to lower the night temperature as the four, drinks in hand, stood together in a circle, drinking, chatting, and generally enjoying each other's company, before heading to their hotel for a final few hours together.

The hotel lounge was comfortable, and despite the packed room and buzz of conversation around them, the women found a relatively private area in which to converse. A waiter took their order and asked about the theatre show, before being called away to serve another customer.

'Tomasz is a lovely guy. He's been so attentive during our stay. He told me about his life in Poland and how much he misses his family,' Liz commented. 'He plans to go back for a visit once the Festival period is over.'

Talk returned to the theatre performance, and before long, Maggie looked at her watch and remarked, 'This has been a wonderful time together. I hate to be a party pooper and break up the happy family, but Letitia and I have an early rise in the morning.'

With hugs and wishes for a safe journey, mother and daughter departed, leaving Julie and Liz to continue their chat. Neither women were early bedders and were content to enjoy each other's company for a few more hours.

'Excuse me a moment, Julie, while I visit the ladies' room,' said Liz, and she headed off, her long, floor-length dress trailing in her wake. Liz had always favoured such long skirts and dresses that reached the ground, but her friends were used to her rather Bohemian style, with beads and such like adorning her unruly hair, and her large spectacles hanging around her neck like a chain of office that inevitably became tangled in her beads and various necklaces. She was one of the kindest people that Julie had ever met, and she blessed the day her fellow school pupil had come into her life. Their friendship was built solidly on trust.

Julie, nursing her drink, let her mind wander to the successful get-together, and vowed to organise another such meeting. Next time we'll plan for a longer stay, she thought. Three days are not nearly enough time together.

Suddenly, she became aware of a figure hovering nearby. It was the man who had accosted her earlier in the street. As he approached her table, she could smell his heavy aftershave and observed how his face seemed tortured and pained.

'Caroline. Please. You have to listen. You need to stop this nonsense. I told you not to come to Edinburgh. What good will it do? We need to talk. We can do this together.' His voice grew louder, as he became more adamant. 'Please don't ignore me after all we've been through.'

By now, he was right in Julie's face, leaning over to get as close as he could.

'Excuse me, whoever you are,' pleaded Julie in a firm tone, but with a modicum of fear, 'please leave me alone. You must be confusing me with someone else. Please leave.'

The man raised his voice again. 'Please, Caroline, don't do this.'

Tomasz, alerted by the tone, came over to the table just as Liz was returning to her seat.

'Are you alright, ma'am?' he asked. 'Is this gentleman annoying you?'

Liz exclaimed, 'That's the guy who shouted at us as we left the theatre.'

The stranger shook his head, shrugged his shoulders and replied, 'It's okay. I'm leaving.' But he turned towards Julie and, with a last comment, added, 'We need to talk Caroline. Please call me.'

With that, he hurried down the carpeted stairway and crossed the hallway, where he was met by the hotel manager who had been alerted by Tomasz.

'Well!' gasped Julie. 'That was a bit scary. Who on earth is he? And why does he think I am someone called Caroline? Thank you, Tomasz, for rescuing me.'

In the foyer, the manager, Geoff Shearer, approached the man. 'Excuse me, sir. May I have a word?'

He beckoned for the man to follow him to a quiet area, away from other guests who were entering the premises.

'Sir,' he continued, 'I believe you have been harassing one of our guests.'

'No, no, that's not it... I only wanted a quiet word with my fiancée, but she's not acknowledging me. I am not harassing anyone, sir. Believe me. I only want to talk to her.'

'Julie Sinclair is your fiancée?' questioned the manager. 'I wasn't aware of that. Ms Sinclair is a regular guest here. I know her well, and if she were planning to be wed, I'm sure she would have told the staff. We have the greatest respect for her.'

'Who is Julie Sinclair?' The man looked confused. 'Sorry, we are talking at cross purposes here. My fiancée is in the lounge; she was with three other ladies. When they left, I took the chance to talk to Caroline privately.'

'Caroline?'

'Yes, Caroline Speirs, my fiancée. She has been staying here for the past few nights with her friends, including the weirdly dressed one who is with her now.'

The manager looked bemused. Julie was a well-known writer, so was he dealing with a besotted fan, or had the man made a genuine mistake? The stranger, equally bemused, reached into his pocket and withdrew a business card, which he handed over.

'Blake Jessop, sir. Here's my card and contact details. I don't understand any of this, but I would appreciate if you would give this to her with my apologies if I have caused any distress. I am totally perplexed. I only want to talk to her.'

The manager accepted the card then signalled for the man to follow him to the reception desk, where he retrieved a business card from a pile in a glass dish.

'This, Mr Jessop, is Julie Sinclair's business card. She is a well-known crime writer. Perhaps she looks not unlike your fiancée, but I assure you we have no-one of the name Caroline Speirs registered her. I pride myself in knowing my guests.'

'And I sir, know my fiancée,' the man replied. 'I don't know what her game is.'

Blake Jessop studied the card again, shook his head in total confusion, then left the hotel and headed out into the cool of the Edinburgh evening.

∞

Packed and ready to head for home, Julie and Liz checked out of the hotel and said goodbye. The receptionist suddenly remembered the business card. 'Oh, I almost forgot to give you this,' she told Julie. 'Mr Shearer left it for you. He looked for you last evening, but you had already retired for the night and he didn't want to disturb you. It was left by the gentleman who spoke to you in the lounge.'

'Oh, thanks, Claudia.' Julie gave the card a perfunctory look before popping it into her jacket pocket.

'Right,' said Liz, 'taxi to the railway station, or walk?'

'Let's walk. The luggage is light enough, but I refuse to carry it down those steps at Fleshmarket Close, or Advocates Close, or any other. And I'm certainly not going down the Waverley steps. We'll go down the longer way.'

Liz laughed at her friend's determination. 'You're usually the fit one. Too much to drink?'

'Well, that and a rather sleepless night. I couldn't get that guy out of my mind. It was quite alarming.' She pulled her collar up around her neck as an imaginary shiver went through her body, filling her with trepidation as she remembered the encounter.

Edinburgh's Old Town brimmed with what was referred to as 'closes' or alleyways – intriguing lanes which wound through the capital, and were normally named after an occupant of the apartments nearby or to a trade that took place there. Fleshmarket Close had once led to a slaughterhouse, the centre of the butcher trade, and was one such alleyway that would take them from their hotel to Waverley railway station where the duo would depart for home.

'That's settled then,' smiled Liz. 'We walk. We have plenty of time before we catch our train.'

The two trundled on, attempting to avoid bumping into Festivalgoers, who seemed to have tripled in numbers from the previous day. Revellers were out in force to soak up the many fringe shows that attracted thousands of artistic and cultural performers from around the globe, making the Edinburgh Festival Fringe the biggest and most popular event perhaps in the world. For three weeks every summer, an explosion of colour, noise, and talent took over the city.

While the two women sat in the station coffee shop waiting for their train to be announced, Liz admired the newly renovated railway station while Julie, with her inquisitive writer's mind, indulged in people watching. Travellers were exiting the trains like a mass evacuation and heading in droves to the capital, their laughter and merriment adding to the already lively atmosphere.

'Where's everyone going?' she mused, mostly to herself, as she hugged her coffee cup and savoured the golden nectar.

'Let's go, girl, our train is here,' interrupted Liz, who had kept her eye on the departure notices. Rummaging in her massive frock pocket for her ticket, she muttered, 'It's here somewhere', eventually locating the important ticket.

They gathered their belongings and made their way through the crowds to the platform and settled into their compartment. Within minutes, the train trundled off towards Fife, and before long crossed the iconic Forth Rail Bridge.

'No matter how many times I cross over this bridge, I am in awe of its structure. And look at the stunning views over the River Forth today,' Julie said, smiling. 'Liz, do you remember when we travelled over here by steam train?'

'Now, that's going back a bit,' her friend laughed. 'But yes, I do remember. Everyone threw a penny out of the window and made a wish.'

'Shame we can't do that now, not with these modern sealed windows. What would you wish for today?'

'Hmm,' Liz replied thoughtfully, taking in the spectacular scene unfolding as the train whisked them over the magnificent structure towards home. 'I would wish for continued health and good fortune for Colin and me to carry on with the business. What about you, Julie? What is your today wish?'

Colin and Liz, with help from her nephew Malcolm, ran a flourishing and successful dog rescue business, Safe Haven, which had faced disaster some years previously when several animals were poisoned. The incident had been an intriguing mystery which the ever-inquisitive Julie had eventually solved.

'I wish to know who the heck Caroline is,' Julie announced firmly. 'She's eating away at my mind.'

Liz laughed. 'Oh, forget the mysterious Caroline. Some crazy guy has mixed you up with a doppelganger. Imagine two Julie Sinclairs!'

Julie chuckled, 'Yes, but one is called Caroline. Oh, look, here we are, almost home.'

Liz's husband Colin met them at the station, hugged both women, loaded the luggage, then headed off for the drive through the East Neuk of Fife and beyond, to home. On the way they told of their visit, their meeting with Maggie and Letitia, and the strange encounter with what Liz termed 'a madman who was after Julie's beautiful body'. Colin laughed at his wife's version of the story and knew she was attempting to bring humour into what must have been a disturbing experience.

The East Neuk, or eastern corner, was made up of several picturesque villages, and not many miles from there was the village of Yetts Bank – home to Colin, Liz, and Julie. A quiet haven off the beaten track, it afforded Julie the peace she craved to get on with her writing.

'Home sweet home,' announced the exhausted writer.

After thanking Colin for the lift, and making arrangements to call around early next day to pick up her two dogs who had been kennelled at Safe Haven, Julie waved her friends off.

Some years before, tragedy had struck at the kennels while Julie and Liz had been attending a book event. Several dogs, including three of Julie's, had been poisoned by a member of the close-knit community – a never-to-be-forgotten event, which even now brought back horrific memories every time Julie drove into the compound.

When her friends drove off, Julie unpacked, lit the log fire to take the chill off the room, then made herself a light supper and settled to read before retiring for the night. She gave a sigh of contentment at being back where she felt content and secure. She was, at heart, a home bird.

∞

Several miles from the peaceful village of Yetts Bank, and many years before Julie's strange encounter, a confrontation had taken place that was to impact on the future life of the writer. The year was 1972, a bleak year in history with the political Watergate scandal in USA and terrorist activity at the Munich Olympics at the forefront of media attention. But none of this was of concern to Cissy Broadbent and her husband, who were involved in a war of words. On the sudden death of her sister, Cissy, who was not at all maternal, felt it her duty to care for Rachel's young son and daughter. Her husband, Harry, was opposed to the idea, as he enjoyed being the sole recipient of Cissy's attention.

'We agreed never to have children,' he told her bluntly, 'so why do you want to spoil the life we have by cluttering it with someone else's kids? Who's going to pay for food and clothes and whatever else kids need?'

'Harry, love, you know I can't abandon Rachel's kids,' Cissy told him. 'What would happen to them? There is no-one else. They are only seven and four years old. We are the only family they have since their so-called father, that waster Todd Jessop, took off to Spain to live with his lover. The terms of the divorce gave Rachel sole custody of the kids, and her loser of a husband is to have no contact – not that he cared a toss about them. The authorities will give us a nominal amount each month to care for them, but they won't need much. I'll see to that.'

Harry snorted grumpily. 'As long as they're not going to be under my feet. I can't stand kids.'

To appease his wife, Harry reluctantly gave in, and for the next decade and more, Rachel's children lived with them in a home where they were fed, clothed, and tolerated, but with no emotional warmth or love. Harry hardly gave them the time of day and, even at an early age, they learned to avoid him.

In their own way, the youngsters rebelled against the strict regime. With no emotional support at home, their school work deteriorated, exacerbated by their absenteeism when stress became intolerable. The youngsters would often leave for school, but not attend classes. They were cunning enough to slip into school as lunch was being served, then slip out again unnoticed. And neither Harry nor Cissy responded to requests from school to discuss the problem children in their care.

The fragile relationship between children and their guardians eventually broke down completely, and soon both teenagers began dabbling in drugs and alcohol, and were expelled from high school. The young boy, in his final year at school, refused to sit exams he had no chance of passing, and left home to fend for himself. His young sister had no choice but to remain at home until she too was old enough to leave. But at the first opportunity, following her brother's actions, she packed her few belongings and left the cold, dismal place that she had loathed all her life.

Blake Jessop moved as far as he could from the Broadbent home, took various jobs to make ends meet and eventually straightened out his life. He joined a Merchant Navy training course, and over a three-year period of cadetship, he proved himself to be a willing pupil. Over the years, and engrossed in his own world of travel, he lost touch with his sister, but she was never far from his mind.

Once, on shore leave, he returned to the Broadbent home to enquire about her.

'We haven't set eyes on her since she stormed out of here a few years after you took off. So much for gratitude after all we did for you both,' muttered Harry Broadbent, returning to his newspaper and dismissing the young man who, holding his temper, refrained from replying.

Reiterating her husband's attitude, Cissy spoke curtly. 'Sorry, Blake, but we have no idea where she is. I'm sure she will be fine. As Harry said, she took off one night without a "thank you for giving me a home" or anything. I found her room empty of clothes, and a load of half-drunk bottles of alcohol stored under the bed. Now, do you want anything else or can I get on with my sewing?'

Knowing he was no longer welcome in the house, Blake returned to his new life. Thoughts of his sister were temporarily put to the back of his mind while he concentrated on his studies which, if successful, would see him advance in his career choice of engineering with the Royal Fleet Auxiliary. He was learning the trade on the job, and had already found his place in the world. He'd made friends among his fellow shipmates and turned his life around – a very different man from the youth who had run from the uncaring and unloving home.

∞

In a squat in a rundown building in a large city, Caroline Jessop shared illegal drugs with other people she thought she knew from somewhere, but it was hard to focus through a haze of confused vision and tremors. Her addiction made her forget her problems – albeit temporarily – but on the rare occasions when she recalled another life somewhere in the dim and distant past, she was unsure why her memories made her angry.

'Good stuff, Caroline,' mumbled a companion as they shared a joint that was passed around a motley crew. One moment they were strangers, at other times, best buddies.

'Make the most of it, Neil,' she replied. 'It's all we have until someone gets some more.'

'I ain't Neil,' replied the guy. 'I'm Hughie.'

'You told me your name was Neil.'

'Did I? I must have got a bit mixed up, I'm sure my name is Hughie.'

'It don't matter none what your name is,' muttered Caroline, as she passed the remains of the joint to him. 'Names don't matter to no-one.' And she promptly fell asleep, dreaming of where the next fix was to come from.

She had already been on a crime spree that week, and had managed to steal a wallet from a gentleman who had placed it on the shop counter while he packed his purchases.

'Hey, you! Come back here,' the distressed man had shouted, but Caroline was off and running to a known dealer.

'Don't worry, Mr Appleton,' reassured the shop owner as he sat the distraught man down and fetched him some water. 'We'll get her. Our cctv has her covered, and I know who she is. She's been banned from this shop, but must have managed to sneak in when my back was turned. She's one of the druggies who live in a squat near the river. The police will pick her up. Meanwhile, let's get you home to Ginty.'

Caroline Jessop had indeed been apprehended, taken to the police station, and charged with theft and possession of a class A drug.

'So, here we are again, Miss. Haven't seen you around for what, at least two weeks? I thought you were a reformed character,' said the receiving officer with a smirk. 'Would you like your usual cell, ma'am? All meals included,' he added, and instructed an officer to escort Caroline Jessop to the cells.

∞

Life in sleepy Yetts Bank continued as normal after the excitement of Julie's visit to the capital.

'I haven't seen you since you got home from Edinburgh. How was the Festival? Did you get to the Military Tattoo at the castle? I've always wanted to attend. I've watched it on tv and promised myself, "Someday, Jessica Morris, you will sit up there and watch the spectacle".'

Jessica, the post office owner and local gossip, hardly paused for breath as she questioned Julie about her recent trip. There wasn't much that Jessica didn't know about the residents of the sleepy hamlet, and she felt it her duty to keep abreast of the coming and goings in her community. 'After all,' she once told a customer, 'people have the right to know what's happening in the village. It makes for good community spirit.'

Julie, finally finding a gap in the incorrigible lady's one-way conversation, replied, 'It was wonderful, Jessica. The city was buzzing with tourists. In fact, with all the different nationalities and languages, it was easy to imagine you were abroad. We had a great time meeting up with friends, and yes, we did manage to get tickets for the Tattoo, which was spectacular. You should decide now about purchasing a ticket for next year, you would be enthralled.'

'Hmm,' commented the invincible Jessica, as she pushed her glasses up onto her head and chewed on the end of her pen. 'It would be lovely, but who would look after the post office and shop in my absence? My duty is here with my community, and as much as I'd like to visit the city, I can't see it happening. Not while I have such an important responsibility here in Yetts Bank.'

'Jessica, surely you are allowed time off? You are entitled to holidays, like everyone else,' said Julie, but she struggled to remember Jessica Morris every taking a break from her beloved post office.

'Well, I was in hospital some years ago, long before you came to Yetts Bank, and you have no idea how much extra work it gave me when I finally returned. I couldn't find a thing; the person they sent to replace me for a month had the place in such an upheaval the likes of which you would never believe. Now, I'm not one to complain, as you know, but nothing was in the correct place.' She shook her head firmly. 'No, as much as I would love a trip to Edinburgh, I could not put myself through all that again. Some people have no idea of order. A place for everything and everything in its place, that's my motto and I stick by it. Now, what was it, Julie, more stamps?'

With Jessica having finished her monologue and suitably vindicated of all faults, Julie took off on her trusted bike to return home to her beloved dogs. They greeted her with their usual exuberance and awaited their titbits while their owner settled to her writing.

As was the norm in Julie's life, no sooner had she begun to write than her cell phone vibrated. She briefly considered ignoring it until she noticed that Maggie was calling. She quickly saved her work on the computer before answering.

'Maggie, how lovely to hear from you.'

'Hi there, Julie, are you busy?' Maggie's Highland lilt had never left her. 'I have some news.'

'Do tell,' replied Julie, curious as to what was making her friend so excited.

'Robin is engaged to his gorgeous Amy-Lee, and they have set a date for the wedding! It's planned around Jonny's holiday, when Parliament is in recess. We are so excited at the prospect of going to California to see our son tie the knot. Letitia is arranging for time off, so it will be a real family gathering. I'm so excited, I can hardly contain my emotions. We've spoken to Amy-Lee by Skype and she's a darling girl. I'm sure Robin has made a good choice.'

'Oh Maggie, I can catch your excitement. Well, the mother of the groom! Who would have believed it?'

'And I don't have a thing to wear.'

Julie laughed as she recalled having a tour of her friend's walk-in dressing room, with its racks full of exquisite clothes, shoes, hats, and accessories. 'Now, if our scatty friend Liz had said that, I would have believed her. But you, Mags dear, have such a choice, and I know you haven't worn even half of that collection.'

'Hmm, I expect you are right. However, I've made arrangements for my personal dresser to visit with some sample outfits. Jonny insists I purchase new for the occasion, so any excuse.'

Julie laughed. She knew that one of Maggie's passions was clothes. 'Good luck with your choice of wedding outfits, and send me pictures. Check what the mother of the bride will be wearing; you don't want to clash. And give my love and congratulations to Robin and his fiancée.'

'I will, my dear. Robin is calling this evening, so I'll pass on your wishes. I guess I'd better leave you to get on with whatever you were doing when I called.'

'I've started writing my autobiography, inspired by the upcoming big birthdays for the three of us,' Julie admitted. 'I thought it was time to take stock of the past and plan for the future. The years are flying by, and I want to capture memories while I still can.'

'That sounds wonderful, and I fully expect to be included – in a nice way, of course. We go back a long time, and thanks for the reminder of the big 5 O.'

'That we do. I still remember when Liz and I joined you in school. We seemed to bond from the start, and here we are, many years later, still the best of buddies,' Julie laughed, and they said their goodbyes.

Now, where was I? muttered Julie to herself as she opened the document on her computer and studied what she had written.

From Reader to Writer, a short autobiography.

It is said that memories, deep in the recess of the brain, are triggered by events that give flashbacks to past occasions: a piece of music perhaps, a photograph, or a chance remark, can set one off on a nostalgic journey. Family tales and accounts of days gone by, as told to us by parents and grandparents, are stored and emerge from the foggy brain when the trigger button is engaged.

How I wish I had listened more to my parents when they recalled their childhood lives and gave a glimpse of the grandparents I never knew. Apart, that is, from my maternal grandmother, who I recall only as a tiny person lying in a recess inset bed, having just passed from this world. I was forbidden to enter that room, but as an inquisitive child even at the tender age of four, I tiptoed in, peeked through the heavy musty curtain that shielded the bed, and touched the cold hand of my first corpse. I remember running and screaming to my mother for comfort, telling her I had seen a spooky ghost. Whether she reprimanded me or not, I cannot recall, but the memory of that event remains with me to this day.

My parents were both only children, so there were no aunts, uncles, or cousins, for me to connect with and I remember being a tad jealous of friends with such relatives and siblings. As an only child, I often wondered what life would have been like if I'd had a companion. I often wished I had a sister; in fact, I longed for a sister. And, as many children do, I invented an imaginary sister whom I called Rebecca.

Although my childhood was happy, I felt something was missing from my life – something I couldn't explain. I had loving parents, though. My mother, the homemaker, taught me to clean, cook, and sew, to her high standards. We had a close relationship and would laugh and giggle at silly things to the tut-tutting from my father, who observed us with a contented smile from behind his newspaper. He was a hard worker – a newspaper editor, who worked long hours and would delight in telling us front page news on the eve of publication. I felt privileged to have inside information, as I saw it. I never tired of hearing about deadlines, special editions, features, and scoops, which seemed to be a race to acquire something of immense importance before other newspapers got hold of it. On a visit as a child to the printing section, I resolved there and then to be a writer.

'Dad. I could write stories for your newspaper, couldn't I?'

My off-the-cuff request was given serious thought and resulted some months later in the inclusion of a children's section. I wrote copious stories and poems, often with illustrations, and was delighted to see my name in print at the age of eight. I encouraged school friends to contribute to the page and, before long, a cluster of children were regular contributors.

It was about that time, when my eight-year-old self was thought to be mature enough to hear from my loving parents that I was adopted. I sat in awe as they gently explained that, as they had no children of their own, they had chosen me to be their special little girl. They painted a picture in my mind of lots of babies lying in a massive room, crying and waiting to be chosen, and I was selected from among them to live with Josephine and Jack Sinclair and given the name Julie Kate, after both grandmothers.

This revelation had little or no emotional effect on me. I was theirs; I was loved, I was happy and continued to thrive under their care. The information that I was adopted was stored away in my brain and seldom surfaced.

I was in my late teens when tragedy struck. My father, attempting to repair an outside light at home, fell from the ladder onto a concrete path. He did not survive. The next few years were emotionally draining, as my previously strong, dependable mother became withdrawn and remote. There was little I could do to bring her out of the darkness of her once happy life.

I will never forget the morning she died. I heard a crash and rushed to the kitchen, only to find my dear mother lying in a heap on the floor. The Procurator Fiscal's report said she would not have felt any pain when her heart stopped. Unbeknown to me, she had been suffering from heart damage for several years. Had it not been for Liz and Maggie, I don't know how I would have coped. I owe a debt of gratitude to these strong women. My only consolation was that my mother had been present at my graduation – the joy on her face was a sight to see, and I treasure the picture of us both taken after the awards ceremony.

School, for me, had been a delight. I thrived in most subjects, but my first love was English language as it was for my forever friends, Liz and Maggie. We often tested each other on our knowledge of grammar, of Shakespeare, Shelley, Burns, and Wordsworth, and many other aspects of the English language. We wrote stories and became each other's critics, devising our own system of editing. This continued at university, where we followed the same degree course. No-one, it seemed, could separate our special trio. There was friendly rivalry among us, and we rejoiced in each other's success.

We followed our dreams, and now, as we each reach a milestone birthday, I look forward with anticipation to the next phase of our lives. Liz, as well as running her animal rescue business, is a book critic whose work I admire. She edits my books professionally, pulls me up as she would any writer, when tiredness leads to carelessness. Maggie, content to write articles for magazines, could not be convinced to write a novel, which I know she is perfectly capable of doing.

Romance flourished for each of us at different times. Liz was the first to tie the knot, when she literally fell at the feet of a fellow student, tripping over the hem of her long frock. Had Colin Grant not caught her, she would have succumbed to serious injuries. Shortly after graduation, the two were wed and moved to Yetts Bank to establish their business. Colin had researched and spotted the ideal place to live and build up Safe Haven, while indulging his passion as a travel writer.

Maggie dated Jonny for several months before discovering he was a mega-rich landowner with political aspirations. Any plans Maggie had on returning to live on her beloved Scottish island were put on permanent hold, and the two married in style and settled to life at Chestermere Hall where, in time, their two children were born and completed the idyllic family unit.

As for me, I dated a few fellow students over the years, but found them hollow and self-centred. Or was I too picky?

'Lighten up, Julie, you frighten guys off with your serious approach to life,' remarked Liz on more than one occasion.

Romance blossomed for me when I visited Liz at Yetts Bank and met Craig Coyle with a group of offshore oil workers in the local pub. We clicked immediately. I found him a deep thinker, a gentleman behind the gruffness so common in the Celtic race, and within a year we were engaged to be married. He had rented a cottage not far from Safe Haven that I shared whenever I visited Liz. My visits became so regular that she suggested I look for property in Yetts Bank.

After much soul searching, I sold my parents' house, moved from the city, and found my own haven of peace where I could indulge my passion for writing as well as being with my lover on his time off. However, with Craig working away from home for weeks on end, we gradually drifted apart. I felt he did not appreciate my work as a writer, seeing it as merely a hobby. On one occasion there was tension between us as I strained to finalise a manuscript that had a deadline looming.

'I'm only home for a few weeks. Can't you forget your writing and let's enjoy each other's company?' he said on more than one occasion.

Things came to a head when he was posted to the Philippines. There, he met and married a local woman, and soon became a father. I bear him no grudge. It would not have worked out for us, as we were too similar in personalities, both strong characters who constantly rubbed each other up the wrong way. We keep in touch, and I was grateful that he was around at a traumatic time when Scamper, the favourite of all my dogs, inadvertently started a series of events that helped solve a major transatlantic crime and led me to rethink my writing genre.

Am I looking for love? I think my answer to myself would be: 'If it comes along, I'll think about it.'

Meanwhile, I continue with life; I enjoy my own company and relish the quietness to write. I have, of course, my dogs. My crazy pooches keep me fit with their insatiable need for walks.

Julie's writing was interrupted by Curly and Topsy edging nearer the door, the latter with his leash in his mouth, ready for a long boisterous walk.

'Okay, you guys. You win. I need fresh air before we settle for the night.' Julie was convinced her dogs understood every word she spoke to them.

∞

The arrival of bulky mailbags caused excitement for the crew, as their ship had been at sea for many months. Most sailors received some form of communication from family and loved ones – letters, parcels, postcards, and photographs. Blake Jessop never received any mail, but sat at the mess table while fellow sailors shared news and the contents of their parcels. At first, he was loathe to intrude and made to leave the room, until his workmates insisted he stay.

On one occasion, Arty – one of the youngest crew members – received a bulky parcel from his doting grandmother, who wrapped every item in newspaper. As news from home was always well received, another crewmate Chunky – so called due to his insistence of wearing two jumpers – spread some of the newspaper pages out on the table and proceeded to inform the crew of events that he could discern from the incomplete sheets.

'Arty, ask your grandmother to send the whole paper,' he laughed as he perused the sports page. 'Ah, rain stopped play at Lords. Arsenal have made another signing – sorry, can't pronounce his name.' And so he continued with his commentary, while others read and shared news from home until interrupted once more by Chunky.

'Hey, Blake, do you know anyone by the name of Caroline Jessop? There's a report here of a court case, a druggie by the sound of it. The page is torn, I can't get any more detail from it.'

He passed the torn newspaper to Blake, who momentarily froze as he looked at the crumpled but unmistakable picture of his dishevelled sister, flanked by police officers. He read as much of the report as was possible, given the state of the paper, then stood to leave. 'Arty, can I have this?'

'Sure,' replied the youth, who was still engrossed in opening parcels.

The crew looked at each other, puzzled at what had transpired. There was no doubt that Blake, a trusted and well-liked mate, seemed deeply affected by the newspaper article.

'Let him be,' insisted Jack, as one of the crew stood to go after him. 'Give him space. I'm sure if he has anything to share, he'll tell us when he's ready.'

Blake took the newspaper to his accommodation, where he spread it out to make it as legible as possible. He read that Caroline Jessop, a homeless person of no fixed address, had been charged with possession of class A drugs and was being held in custody, awaiting sentencing. Blake could not make out the date on the paper but knew it must be from several months ago, as mail to the ship was spasmodic. He drew an intake of breath, sighed, and wiped a tear from the corner of his eye as he thought of the little sister he had loved and protected from the harsh regime they had been living in.

How did it get to this? Poor Caroline. I could have helped you, if you'd left with me when I decided enough was enough in the Broadbent house. I should have insisted that you come with me.

For the next hour, Blake thought of nothing else but vulnerable, troubled Caroline. Making out the name of the court, he fired off an email to the Sheriff, identifying himself as the older sibling of the accused, and asking for information about her court case. He explained that he was at present on a tour of duty, but would return home soon to discover the court's findings. He did not elaborate on their home circumstances, but merely touched on how difficult life had been to cause them both to leave home in their late teens.

Blake was unsure if he would receive a reply. He clicked send just as the warning bell summoned him to his watch.

For the next four hours, he concentrated fully on his job, pushing Caroline and her troubles temporarily to the back of his mind.

∞

The prison regime that Caroline Jessop found herself in was harsh but much better than living in a cold, damp squat with a motley crew of misfits from a society that appeared to have turned its back on its most vulnerable citizens. She shared a cell with two other women, so space was at a premium, and she was ordered not to intrude on Fiona Elder's patch.

Fiona appeared to be the matriarch of the women's wing. Everyone deferred to her and felt favoured when signalled out to tend to the needs of the goddess. She was a large lady with a loud voice and manner that would intimidate some inmates. Caroline's other cellmate was a woman about her own age, who tried to help the terrified newcomer.

'First time in jail?' enquired Shirley, as she helped Caroline make her bed and store her meagre possessions.

'Yes,' Caroline whispered, still recovering from the shock of a prison sentence. She had expected to be given community service.

'Just keep your head down and do what big Fiona asks, or life could be even more scary,' Shirley advised. 'She's all talk, bluster, and blowing, but underneath there's a heart of gold. Best to keep out of the way as much as possible. Stick with me and I'll show you the ropes. First things first. When did you last have a shower? You stink.'

'Dunno,' replied Caroline rather sheepishly. She was unaware that her body odour was offensive.

'Don't suppose you have any toiletries? You can borrow mine for now until you earn enough to buy your own. Have you been given a job yet? We all work at something to earn a few pounds.'

Shirley talked on, asking questions, but her confused new cellmate was struggling with the effects of addiction and trying to comprehend how she had found herself here, sharing a prison cell with the fearsome Fiona woman.

'Right, let's get you to the shower room. I'll hang around and keep watch,' Shirley said. 'You can't be too careful here. Bring the clean togs they gave you, and wash your dirty things in the shower. It's the best you can do until we get you a laundry slot.'

Caroline's head was buzzing with Shirley's instructions, but the shower revived her spirits. The fragrance from the gel made her feel more human than she had for some time, and cleaner than she had for many months. Shirley watched over her during the next few weeks, making sure the newbie did not become an easy target for bullying. Knowing the newbie shared a cell with Fiona, most inmates gave her a wide berth, afraid they might face the wrath of the matriarch if Caroline mentioned she was being ill-treated.

As part of her sentencing, Caroline had to take part in a drug awareness and rehabilitation programme, and was shocked to discover that her two cellmates were part of the team, which was composed of a therapist, a prison warden, and prisoners who had coped with cold turkey and were now drug-free.

Fiona looked at Caroline and, for the first time since they met, smiled as she said, 'You didn't expect to see me here, did you?'

Fiona explained to the small group that her life had been blighted by drugs from an early age. She related that her father had been a dealer, so drugs were freely handed out among the family. She lost two brothers in their early twenties, and a sister in her teens – all to drugs. The father was an abuser, a foul-mouthed man, who met his end when attacked and knifed by addicts who thought he had shortchanged them.

'I wasn't sorry when he died,' Fiona admitted to the group. 'I didn't shed any tears. He was a brute, but by that time I was hooked on heroin and anything else I could get my hands on. My life was a mess and I ended up in here for a long stretch. As for my mother, she walked out on us and hasn't been heard of since. This programme that you are all on turned my life around. I'm clean now, and when I'm released in three months from now, I'm going to train as a counsellor to help others get out of the misery that drugs can do to your mind.

'So, you guys,' she went on, glaring at each of the inmates in turn, 'listen up to one who's been down there, right in the gutter. Get all the help you can from this programme, listen to the team, get yourself off the stuff, and change your life around. You only have one chance at life, so grab it with both hands. If you're down there in the pits of hell, like I was, the only way is up. It is never too late to change the course of your life. We can help, but you need to want to change.'

Her words had a profound effect on Caroline, and she was determined to get clean of her addiction. Fiona was not as scary as she'd first thought, and talked with her well into the night. Shirley, too, had been an addict. With help from the rehab programme and encouragement from Fiona, she had weaned herself off all drugs and reconnected with her middle-class family who, through embarrassment, had previously abandoned her to her fate. She was also due for release.

Fiona had probed Caroline about her family and life with the Broadbents.

'I've got no-one now since Blake left home,' Caroline admitted. 'I don't even know where he is. I wish I did.'

'Why don't you write to them and ask if they have a contact address? It might be your only chance at finding him,' encouraged Shirley. 'I'll help you compose it if you like.' She knew from previous conversations that Caroline was ashamed of her lack of literary skills.

Much to the disgust of the Broadbents, a letter marked HMP duly arrived at their home.

'Told you so. I told you she'd come a cropper someday,' smirked Harry Broadbent, as his wife read the letter. 'I told you we should never have taken Rachel's brats in, but did you listen to me? No, and look where it's got us, the laughing stock of the street when her face was all over the papers.'

'So you keep telling me, Harry, but I had to do some-thing for my sister's kids,' Cissy snapped back. 'And yes, I'm ashamed to be associated with them now, especially her. The cheek of writing to us on prison paper; you know what that postman is like, a real gossip. There won't be a soul in the street who doesn't know we've had a letter from prison.'

Harry shrugged. 'I suggest you ignore it.'

Cissy sighed, shook her head, and put the envelope with the letter behind the mantelpiece clock, hoping to forget about it. But a few days later, with her conscience troubling her, she sent a curt reply:

Caroline Jessop, I have no idea where your brother is. He came back here a year ago looking for you, then he went back to his ship. He's in the Merchant Navy and that's all I know about him. Do not contact us again. You are no blood relative of mine. I only took you in out of sympathy for my foolish sister, who had the stupidity to adopt you both – you're not even brother and sister. Sort your life out, but don't include me in it. Cissy Broadbent.

Caroline was stunned as she read the short note from her former guardian, and shared it with her cellmates. They'd grown to care for their confused inmate in their own way.

'I can't get my head around the fact that Blake and me are not brother and sister. Why did no-one ever tell us? I wish I knew where he was; he might have some answers for me.'

That night, Caroline sobbed into her pillow as she relived her past life where love had been replaced with indifference, and where her brother – as she still thought of him – had been her strength and support through difficult times.

∞

Blake had not expected a reply to his email from the court, so was surprised and delighted some months later when a file attachment arrived, giving an account of court proceedings for Caroline Jessop. The newspaper that Arty's grandmother had used to wrap his gifts in, turned out to be four months old.

He read that his sister had pled guilty to possession and, as a first offender, was sentenced to twelve months in prison and ordered to attend a drug rehabilitation course. By the time he was due for shore leave, Caroline would be more than halfway through her stretch in prison. He had some plans to make.

He was elated at finally having a contact address for her, even if she was under the care of HMP service. It's a start, he thought.

Feeling it only right to explain, he shared his news with his crew friends.

'You guys have been great at leaving me to sort out the distressing news about my sister without probing for information,' he told them. 'I've some news I want to share. It's only right, as you've put up with my long face for months now. Caroline and I had a dreadful upbringing with an aunt and uncle, after our mother died. They never wanted us there, and to this day I wonder why they bothered taking us in... Anyway, it was so bad that I left home as soon as I could when I was seventeen, and lost touch with my sister who left home a few years after me.

'She got herself into a mess with drugs and alcohol and ended up in prison,' he went on. 'That was the article in Arty's newspaper that upset me. But I've now got information as to where she's being held, and I plan to make contact when we next have shore leave. I'm hoping to help her sort out her life.'

His mates let him talk and unburden himself, and wished him well in his plan to visit his sister when his shore leave was granted.

∞

Fiona Elder's release from prison was almost party-like, with inmates gathering to wish her well. A few, including Shirley and Caroline, added their thanks for helping them turn from addiction. It was not long before her place was filled by another prisoner – Rose, who spent most of her time either sleeping or crying. She was a single mother whose children had been taken into care when it became obvious that she was unfit, through her addiction, to care for them.

A few weeks later, Shirley was released from prison and promised to keep in touch.

'It won't be long now,' she said reassuringly, 'until you're walking out of here and we'll meet up.' She had helped Caroline through the devastating news that she was adopted.

Without Blake to guide her, the girl felt utterly alone in the world.

Seeing her friend descending into depression, Shirley had tried to help her devise a plan for her release from prison.

'What is the first goal for you?'

'When I get out of here, I need to find somewhere to live and get a decent job,' Caroline replied.

'And then what?' encouraged Shirley.

Caroline moaned silently and sighed. Her voice quivered as she said, 'I want to find out who I am.'

'Right, kid,' Shirley told her, 'keep that to the front of your mind.'

∞

Caroline was working in the prison kitchen when she was called to the visitors' hall. She occasionally had visits from her solicitor or social worker, so expected this to be one of them.

'Tidy yourself up, Jessop,' instructed the warden who summoned her. 'You don't want to scare off your handsome visitor.'

Bemused and not a little curious, she entered the visitors' hall, which was already busy with family and friends. Looking around, she saw a suntanned man smiling and waving to her.

'Over here, Caroline!' called Blake.

Stunned and elated, she threw herself into his arms and wept on his shoulder, until a warden told them to break away. Once composed, they sat together holding hands, just content to be in each other's company again after so long.

'Don't cry, Caroline,' Blake said eventually. 'I'm here for you now, and I'll take care of you. I didn't know where you were, but I thought about you often.' He related his life as a seaman and explained how a chance piece of newspaper had led him to her.

Through eyes red with crying, she spoke of her life as it spiralled downwards into the mire leading her to her present state.

'I'm clean now, Blake, no more drugs for me,' she assured him. 'I've learned my lesson. Of all places to learn it, it was here in prison.'

Visiting time flew by, and there was still much more the two wanted to talk about.

'I'll be back as soon as they allow me to visit,' he said, 'and I'll write to you often. Keep strong. It won't be long until you walk out of here.' He smiled. 'We have so much planning to do.'

She nodded and she turned to leave, then faltered slightly. 'Blake,' she began, 'we're not related. We're not brother and sister. Did you know that?'

Moved on by a warden who indicated visiting was over, Blake had no time to reply. He hunched his shoulders as he ventured out into the chill of the day, his mind in a quandary as to what Caroline's passing remark could possibly mean. Not brother and sister? How could that be? We belonged to Mum and Dad, Rachel and Todd Jessop. I don't understand.

A day or two later, and after sleepless nights, he phoned the Broadbents for clarity. As he dialled the number, his stomach churned at the prospect of another rejection from the people who'd been their guardians during his childhood. He only had vague memories of life before he went to stay with them.

The phone was picked up by Harry, who wasted no time in letting Blake know that his call wasn't welcome.

'Please, I just want to ask one question,' pleaded Blake, his hand sweating as he gripped onto the telephone receiver.

'Ask, and be quick about it,' Harry grumbled.

'Are Caroline and I blood relatives?'

The curt reply stunned him. 'You are not related. Rachel and Todd adopted you separately, three years apart, and there's no relationship. Bet you're glad you've not got a sister as a jailbird,' Harry Broadbent chuckled as he ended the call.

∞

Julie's walk with her dogs took longer than expected, veering off on a path that took them further into the woods and even further from home. She sighed as she allowed them the freedom to run and play-fight, oblivious to the steady rain that threatened to become a torrential downpour. A storm was forecast, and she wanted home before it began in earnest.

This particular route reminded her of her walk several years ago with Scamper, whose inquisitiveness had led him to fall into an old, long forgotten pit shaft, but it was one of her favourite places where the dogs had freedom to roam.

Eventually, called to heel, the dogs shook themselves dry, albeit over her, before heading for shelter and home. Fed and watered, they settled by the fire, ignoring their owner as she got on with the business of preparing her own supper.

During the night, the storm raged in earnest. Julie woke with a start when she heard water running somewhere in the house. The storm had knocked out the electricity supply, and Julie swore as she bumped into furniture while she fumbled for a flashlight. Oh no, the battery is dead. I meant to buy a replacement.

Stumbling downstairs, she almost tripped over the dogs. Wakened by the noise, they were up and ready for fun. A quick glance out of the window confirmed that the entire street was in darkness. At least it's not just my supply that's off, she thought.

Rummaging around, she found some candles and matches. Soon she had enough light to locate the steady plop of dripping water; it was coming from the roof, into the attic, and down into her bedroom. She tentatively and dangerously climbed into the attic with only a candle to guide her. Oh no, it looks like some tiles have blown off, she groaned inwardly, as she observed a chink of light through a gap.

Gingerly, she climbed back down to collect some bowls to catch the steady flow of water until daylight came and she could see what damage had been done. For the rest of the night, she dozed by the fire, knowing she would have little sleep with the constant drip of water disturbing her rest.

Julie was wakened suddenly by someone banging on her door. She had slept better than expected, and was startled by the loud voice from Jack Denny, her neighbour.

'Julie. There's been some damage to your roof. Tiles have been blown off and are lying in the garden. I'll fetch a ladder and some tarpaulin to cover it as a temporary measure until you can have it repaired. There's been a lot of damage during the night, and there's no electricity anywhere. People are gathering in the village hall where there's some form of heat.'

The two spoke briefly before Jack, with help from one of the other neighbours, set about covering the roof.

'That should do it for the moment,' he said as he inspected his handiwork.

Julie climbed back up into the attic where the container holding the rainwater was not quite full. *That's a relief that it hasn't overflown.*

As she turned to make her way down, she spotted a large trunk that she had brought from her parents' house. *I'd forgotten about that stuff... hmm... must get around to seeing what's in there... someday.*

She dressed quickly, donned a warm jacket, then let the dogs out into the garden for a quick run around. Neither dog lingered too long and returned to their corner of the house, after being fed. Julie joined the other anxious villagers in the hall, where the caretaker had lit portable heaters and provided welcome warm drinks.

'I can always rely on this old gas cooker. To think the committee wanted to have it replaced with a new-fangled electric thing. Where would we be tonight without a cup of tea?' he said as he glowered at a few of the committee who were warming themselves by a heater.

Later in the day, most of the villagers returned to their homes to inspect the damage. *First things first, I need to get batteries for the torch,* Julie thought, as she cycled uphill to the post office which also served as a village shop. The incorrigible Jessica, warmly dressed in an outdoor coat with her woollen hat pulled tightly over her head, smiled as Julie joined a queue for her attention.

The shop was lit by a paraffin lamp that gave a warm glow to the place, allowing Jessica enough light to see by. She was in her element relating her version of the storm and tut-tutting as one customer after another enquired about candles, flashlights, and batteries.

'People need to be prepared for such eventualities,' she scolded. 'It doesn't do to leave essential items until the last minute when there's a run on my stock with no possibility of me getting an order in for several days. People should think ahead.'

Duly chastised, Julie set off for home with a pocket full of batteries and, as a precaution, another large flashlight.

Raymond Newton, another of Julie's neighbours and good friend, was waiting for her at the door. 'Jack told me you have some tiles loose. Do you need me to have a look in the attic at the damage?'

'Oh, please. Yes, do come in.'

The two climbed into the attic space and Raymond began emptying the water from the container.

'Ingenious,' declared Julie. as her neighbour, using a large jug, proceeded to empty the contents jug by jug by pouring it out of the small attic window onto the garden path. 'We'll have to stop meeting like this,' she said, and they both laughed.

Some years before, when Raymond and his family arrived in the village, they had moved into an old house and found a treasure trove of stolen goods in the attic. The inquisitive Julie had helped instigate the investigation into a long-forgotten heist.

'While you're here, Raymond,' she asked, 'could you give me a hand to take this old trunk downstairs? I really must go through my parents' things and see if anything is worth keeping.'

With a bit of manoeuvring, hampered by the playful dogs who had managed to escape from their part of the house, the leather trunk was finally deposited in the sitting room. With grateful thanks to Raymond and a promise to pop in and visit Mary and the children, Julie turned her attention to the needs of the dogs.

The battery lamp that she had purchased, and the glow from the fire, gave the sitting room a cosy ambience. Julie sat on the floor by the fire, a glass of her favourite wine nearby, and opened the trunk. For the next few hours, she reminisced on her early life, and learned something of her parents' past. She pored over photographs – some faded with age; some of people she didn't know – and smiled as she recalled childhood memories captured now in print. She discarded some pictures and paperwork, and was almost ready to call it a night when she spotted a large brown envelope. It was sealed and marked: Private. This letter is for Julie Kate Sinclair.

Julie recognised her father's distinctive handwriting, and was about to open the faded envelope when a cheery voice and barking dogs interrupted her.

'Cooee! It's only us. Friends bearing gifts.'

Liz, her hair in its usual tangled mess and carrying a casserole, came into view, followed by Colin bearing two bottles of wine. 'We thought with you not having electricity, we could have supper together. We have our own small generator, which has been a life-saver. Chicken casserole anyone?'

The three enjoyed a pleasant evening. Colin had brought along his guitar, and the two women listened as he expertly worked the strings.

'That beats clearing out a trunk any day,' declared Julie, as she explained why she was surrounded by paperwork. 'I was just about to open this letter when you arrived. Hold on while I read it. I'm intrigued.' She donned her glasses, pushed her hair out of her eyes, and perused the contents of the envelope.

'Julie,' Liz ventured, noticing her friend's change in demeanour, 'are you okay? You look pale.'

Julie looked up from the letter she held in her hands and was silent for a time. 'It's about my adoption that I've never given much thought to. This paperwork gives some details. Oh goodness. Liz, Colin, listen to this. I'm Irish. Born in Scotland to Irish parents from Galway. Mother named as Orla Coogan, father named as William Hanrahan, an estate ranger. I was given the name Kathleen. Wow.' The paper shook as she held it in her hands, reading and re-reading as if she couldn't quite process what she was seeing. 'And there's another note, a handwritten letter from my mum.'

Julie cleared her throat and began reading aloud,

'Julie, darling Julie, your dad and I want you to have this information, should you ever feel inclined to discover your origins. We know that being adopted did not cause you any distress; you were our little girl, our pride and joy. Had you asked, we would have given you this information, but decided to withhold it until required. All we were told by the adoption agency was that your birth mother came from a very wealthy Irish family, the cream of Irish society. You have our blessing to pursue this...'

Julie folded the paper and kept the rest of the contents to herself. She was visibly stunned.

Liz commented, 'Well, well, what a turn up. Here we have it, our very own Irish colleen. You've gone quite pale, my dear. That's quite a revelation. Are you going to investigate your Irish background?'

Julie shook her head. 'No. I've no interest in this. I'm me. I'm happy with my life, so why disturb things?' she said, as she replaced the letter in the envelope.

Colin laughed. 'But, Julie, you could be rich, the heir to grand castle.'

Julie gave a short laugh as she attempted to change the subject. 'Let's have some more wine before you two have me packed off to the Emerald Isle. I've more important things to attend to, like having the roof fixed. And I've some work to do on my book. Colin, you can go hunt down leprechauns if you like, but don't involve me in your dreams of castles in the air. We already have a Lady in our group, our Lady Maggie, so another titled Lady would give poor Liz an inferiority complex.' Julie held out her glass for a top-up of her favourite wine.

Sensing her need to discuss other matters, Colin asked, 'Do you have insurance cover to fix the roof and the water damage in your bedroom? Knowing you, my dear, it will not have been renewed.'

Julie frowned. 'I'm sure I have. Let me have a rummage around in the bureau.'

Her friends waited as she rustled through mounds of paper. Neither held out much hope of her having the important insurance cover.

'Hmm, eureka! And it is up to date, Colin. Ye of little faith. I'll get in touch tomorrow and make arrangements for the assessor to visit.'

Before leaving for home, Liz offered Julie and her pets accommodation at Safe Haven until the work was complete.

'Thanks, guys, tempting though it is, I'd rather be on site. Anyhow, I have this trunk to sort out, so that will keep me busy.'

Colin gave her a peck on the cheek. 'Now, don't you go off to Ireland without telling us,' he joked.

After her final walk of the evening, she settled the dogs for the night and resumed her reading of the contents of the trunk, including the letter about her adoption. As sleep called, she closed the lid and stored the case in a space under the stairs.

∞

Blake corresponded regularly with Caroline and related his brief conversation with Harry Broadbent. Both he and Caroline were bemused at the revelation that they were not blood relatives. Why did no-one tell us? they asked regularly in letters to each other.

Having him back in her life gave Caroline the incentive she needed to think positive thoughts about her future. With only a few months left of her sentence, she agreed to his suggestion that he should find a place for them to rent. He intended to leave the Merchant Navy and hone his engineering skills in civvie street. He was also motivated to provide a home for them both, to secure employment, and to help Caroline adjust to life out of prison, free from addiction.

Meanwhile, she made use of the prison library and spent hours improving her reading and writing skills, and perusing books on adoption law. I'm determined to find out who I am, and of course, who Blake is.

In one of her letters to him, she informed him that she was considering changing her name by deed poll:

'I've looked into it, Blake, it seems easy to do and I want rid of the name Jessop. It never really belonged to me. I'm going to call myself Caroline Speirs, for no other reason than I like the name, until such times as I find my birth name. I'm changing my name by deed poll.'

'I'm fine with that,' was his reply as he continued to research suitable jobs.

He spent several hours online searching for employment and was delighted to have an initial Zoom interview with a company in Scotland, followed by a face-to-face meeting at which he was offered a promising position to begin in four weeks' time. He felt happier than he had been for several years as he headed to a housing association office that he had researched. There, a helpful lady took details and produced a few pages of potential rental apartments that were ready to move into, and showed him those nearest to where he would be working.

'You might want to consider these two, both in the same apartment block, within easy walking distance to your place of work and a stone's throw from the shopping area and transport links,' she said. 'Both have immediate entry, on payment of a deposit and completion of paperwork. I can arrange for viewing tomorrow morning with Gerry our estate officer.'

Blake could barely contain himself as he left the office and headed to the hotel where he had reserved a room for a few nights. And the viewing with Gerry the following day was not disappointing. An affable forty-something man with a wealth of knowledge of his trade, he expertly showed Blake around both apartments, pointing out the pros and cons of each.

'Apartment twelve is south facing and away from the buzz of traffic; it has the advantage of a little balcony that leads from the sitting room. Apartment sixteen, on the other hand, while slightly bigger is a tad noisier, being near the bus hub. It's a matter of personal choice, sir.'

Blake had no hesitation in accepting tenancy of apartment twelve, and arranged to call at the office to finalise arrangements.

Returning to his temporary living accommodation in a rather rundown area within easy reach of the prison, he arranged for a final visit to Caroline to show her pictures of the apartment and the area where they were to live.

'I'm going back to freshen up the rooms,' he explained. 'Look at these paint cards and help me choose.' Two heads close together perused the cards and, after much deliberating, chose colour schemes for each of the rooms.

'I'll be back on your release date to pick you up and head to our new home – and freedom,' he told her. 'How are you progressing with the change of name? I guess if you go ahead with it, I'll have to get used to calling you Caroline Speirs.' He smiled as he noticed how much his sister had relaxed since his first visit. He had always protected her from the harsh regime with the Broadbents, and felt a surge of love as he looked at her.

'Progressing well,' she replied. 'Pete, the social worker here, has been researching things for me, so I just I need the full address now of our new place for him to continue. Once I have the official deed of poll, there are various agencies to notify. Pete will give me a list of them. I need some kind of photographic identity; he suggests a passport. Will I need one? Will we ever go abroad?'

Caroline was excited at the prospect of a new life, a new name, a new city, and hopefully a new job. 'He's also dealing with the adoption research, and said it was the most complicated case he had ever come across, but he hopes to have made inroads before my release.'

'Why shouldn't we go abroad?' Blake laughed. 'I've seen so many wonderful places, I want to show some of them to you. Yes, go ahead with the passport. Do you need money?'

'Pete said he'll see to it and send an account when everything is in place. I have some money from my meagre prison pay. I'm so excited. I'm crossing off the days until I can turn my life around. Thank God you found me.'

Caroline's release day was joyful. Blake met her at the gate in a second-hand car that he had purchased, and drove her away from the area to begin a new life.

'So, Caroline, my little sister. What do you want to do first?'

She laughed. 'I have a bucket list. Can we go somewhere where I can have a shower and get the stink of prison off me? Then I want to eat a proper meal, something very different from prison mush... then I want to buy fresh clothes and burn these horrid ones that are not fit for purpose... then I want to have my hair and nails done, and have a passport picture taken, and start applying for employment... then—'

Blake threw his head back and roared with laughter. 'Oh Caroline... you haven't changed a bit. You always had plenty to say. Yes, we'll head for town where we'll do some clothes shopping and get you to a hairdresser and photobooth. I'll book us into a hotel where you can shower, change, and have a proper meal. How does that sound?'

It felt a little strange being with the man who, until a few months ago, she had thought of as her brother. But Caroline smiled with admiration at him, as she replied, 'Just wonderful, just wonderful.' Then she rolled the car window down, letting the breeze and fresh air she had been so deprived of for months waft over her, as she closed her eyes and pictured her new life.

The next few months were spent with the former siblings reconnecting, growing closer and, unknown to the other, slowly falling in love. Caroline Speirs, as she now called herself, obtained employment in a local shop and spent her lunch break in the nearby library, where she discovered a suppressed love of reading. It had been denied to her as she grew up in a house where reading a book was deemed as idleness. The irony of Harry Broadbent spending hours perusing his newspaper was not lost on her. Rules for some, she had thought, as she kept the unfairness of it to herself.

Blake enjoyed his new position with his firm, worked diligently, and was a popular and reliable employee. He was happier than he had ever been. He sent up a prayer of thanks to Arty's grandmother, who had unknowingly brought him to an exciting new phase in his life.

He enjoyed his role as unofficial mentor to Caroline. Although he was comfortable around her, his feelings for her confused him somewhat as he still considered himself to be her older brother.

Those feelings came to a head one evening as they both tidied the kitchen after their meal. As Caroline lifted a plate to put it away, their eyes met and locked in an understanding that something stronger than sibling love was emerging.

'Blake...'

'Caroline...'

Words were not necessary as they kissed for a long time, before moving to the bedroom for a night of suppressed passion. Tears of relief and joy, mixed with euphoria, sealed their love and saw them begin a new and fulfilling chapter in their lives. The former siblings had become lovers.

Blake, keen to formalise their relationship, asked Caroline to marry him.

'I want to take care of you for the rest of our lives. We are meant to be together,' he told her. 'Please say you will be my wife.'

Caroline smiled, a wise, contented smile. 'I'll follow you to the ends of the earth if we can be together. Of course I will marry you, but...'

Her hesitation scared him as he waited for the 'but' to be explained.

'I do not want to become Mrs Jessop. Jessop is not your name any more than it is mine. I got rid of it and don't want to use it again. It means nothing to me. Let's get engaged. I don't want to be married until we both find out who we really are. Does that sound selfish? Blake, I need to know who we are.'

Blake held her in his arms, savouring the fragrance from her perfume, and whispered, 'Of course we can wait. You are not being selfish, just surprisingly practical. Tomorrow we will go shopping for a ring.'

∞

With her roof duly repaired and her bedroom redecorated, Julie turned her attention to the rest of the house that had been untouched since she moved in several years ago. She had always intended to tackle the decorating and now, impressed by the light and airy bedroom that had been given a facelift, she decided, Right. I'll seize the moment and have the entire house decorated.

The next few weeks became a frenzy of activity as she cleared room after room to allow the decorators to proceed, and made several trips to the local recycling centre. At one point, Jessica Morris popped out of her post office to enquire, 'Julie, what is going on down there at your house? I see several decorator vans – not that I'm complaining about the parking or anything like that. You know I'm very toler- ant of strangers arriving in the village. Are you doing up your place to sell? Are you moving on? You know we would miss you if you left Yetts Bank.'

Julie smiled inwardly as she replied, 'No, Jessica. I'm not moving out. I'm having the entire house decorated room by room. It's time it was seen to.'

Jessica returned to her work, shaking her head as if she was disappointed in Julie's reply. How she would have loved to be the custodian of news that Julie Sinclair was selling up and moving from Yetts Bank.

Joe the decorator, enjoying a break and a cup of tea with Julie, asked about the trunk stored under the stairs. 'I need to move it,' he said. 'Where do you want it put for safety?'

'I'd forgotten about that trunk.' Julie looked thoughtful. 'It's quite heavy and I need to clear some things from it. Would you be kind enough to lift it onto the dining room table, and I'll go through things in there.'

It was several more weeks before the work was finally completed, but when Julie glanced around her newly refurbished home, she declared it well worth the effort. She had invited some friends for dinner – a belated house-warming event – and planned her menu with care, catering for her guests' individual tastes in food.

With the day fast approaching, all that was required was that she set the table early, to avoid interrupting her cooking.

Oh, no. That trunk needs moved again.

Rather than carry the heavy container to another room, she sat at the table, opened the trunk once more, and was ruthless in discarding photographs of people she never knew and documents and paper clippings that were of no interest to her. What a pair of hoarders you two were. She smiled at the memory of her parents. Once more, she came across the letter addressed to her and re-read it. Do I want to be bothered chasing this up? she sighed, as she replaced it in the envelope and put it behind the dresser clock.

With the trunk almost empty, she placed it under the stairs where it remained for several years, forgotten and unwanted. The letter too, languished behind the clock, gathering dust as the months rolled by.

∞

Urged on by Caroline's determination to find their roots, and anxious to wed his sweetheart, Blake began research to find his birth origin. Should he succeed and discover his true family name, the way would be clear for marriage. An online search of adoption agencies filled him with dread as he scrolled down the various different organisations. He had no adoption certificate, no official record of his birth, and his request to the Broadbents to locate it had resulted in further rejection.

'Don't you ever give up pestering us? We don't have such a document,' said Cissy curtly. 'My sister never showed me any paperwork when she adopted you. All I know is that you were born somewhere in Scotland.'

Armed with that fragment of information and his date of birth, he fired off several emails to a selection of adoption agencies and societies, then waited. It only resulted in some negative replies and a few helpful suggestions as to where else he could take his request.

As the weeks passed, Caroline began to think he was no longer interested in finding out about his beginnings in life, until one evening he arrived home from work fired with enthusiasm and waving a print-off from a reply he had received.

'Caroline. I've been asked to fill in this form and give as many details as I can, which isn't much, but I feel hopeful. Why would these people contact me if they didn't have some information about me?'

The two put their heads together as they perused the form.

'How exciting,' she said. 'Let's get this filled in and hopefully set the ball rolling. I have my heart set on a dress that I saw in a shop window, and there's flowers to be arranged, and a photographer to hire and...'

Blake chuckled at her eagerness to plan their wedding. 'And wedding rings to buy,' he added, as he completed the paperwork.

More weeks passed before he was contacted by a case worker who, if required, would guide him through the maze of research material. He spoke by phone with Hettie Moore, the case worker, who warned him of the possibility of perhaps never finding his birth parents, and of rejection and dashed hopes.

'I don't want to sound negative, Blake, I just want you to be prepared for all eventualities. Not all birth parents, for whatever reason, want to be found.'

'I fully understand,' he replied, 'and I'm prepared for failure, but at least I must attempt to find out who I really am. My future depends on this.' He warmed to the case worker and told her briefly about his wish to marry Caroline.

'Good, then let's go ahead. We need a DNA sample from you, then I can check out the excellent database that we have been told is the best in the world. I'll send you the kit and instructions as to how to go about it. It may take some time to get a result for you, though, as there are thousands of samples to be checked. And, as I have said, there may not be anyone who matches your DNA. However, let's try to unlock your past.'

Time seemed to stand still for the couple as they anxiously awaited the results. Blake tried to encourage Caroline to take the first steps into finding her own past, since it was she who was adamant that she needed to know who she was.

'I will do, but not until you have your results,' she told him. 'Let's sort out one of us at a time. I don't think I could cope with any more stress at the moment. I'm scared for you that this will end in failure.'

She was alone at home when an official-looking envelope dropped onto the doormat, addressed to Blake. This could be what we are waiting for. She paced up and down the apartment, the clock hands seeming to move slowly as she counted the hours until Blake would return. Her mind flitted from thoughts of euphoria if the news was good, and despondency if not. Hearing his key in the door and his cheery, 'I'm home,' she threw herself into his arms.

'Missed me that much,' he laughed, as he pulled her to him. He could hear her heart racing.

'It's come, the letter has come. I've been looking at the envelope all day, just willing you to come home.'

They sat together as he nervously slid it open. His hands were trembling and sweat began to form on his brow as he read the detailed result and cover letter from Hettie.

'Darling. I have a match,' he whispered. 'Oh my gosh. I'm matched with four people.' He rubbed his brow, wiped a falling tear, and re-read the document. 'Oh, I have two half-brothers, a half-sister and... gosh... my birth mother. All still alive. Hettie is going to call me this evening. Caroline, my birth mother is alive, I'm shaking all over.'

The two wept in each other's arms, elated at the news and apprehensive as to what would happen next. 'I have a real family out there. Caroline, I'm shaking with excitement and I admit to being fearful.'

The last of the autumn glow faded from the window, and Caroline lit some candles that they preferred to use instead of glaring electric light. She had prepared an easy supper that they ate from the little table where Blake had left his mobile phone to catch Hettie's call.

After they'd eaten, he paced anxiously up and down, holding his phone tightly in his hands until sweat settled on the instrument. He checked and rechecked his battery power, his connection, and stared at it as if willing it to ring. When it did, he jumped with fright as he pressed 'accept'.

'Blake,' said the now familiar voice of Hettie. 'How are you this evening?'

He wanted her to dispense with pleasantries and get to the crux of the matter, which she did without much ado.

'You will see from the result that you have four living relatives, including your birth mother, who it appears, has been trying to contact you. Her details were left with us should anyone make enquiries. We are not allowed to disclose information until the other person gives permission, and I'm pleased to say there is some information here that I can give to you.'

Hettie paused to let the news sink in. It was a momentous moment for him. She had dealt with clients who were devastated when disappointment set in and euphoria when families were reconnected.

Blake stuttered a reply, 'What happens now?'

'If you agree, I will contact your birth mother and ask for contact to take place. This will be her choice, to write to you, or call, text, or whatever she sees fit. It will be a tremendous step for her to take, too.'

'Please do. Now we've got this far, I would like to hear from her. What can you tell me about her?'

'She is Elisabeth Carter, to her maiden name, but married Lionel Shepley and calls herself Lisa Shepley. I won't give you any more information, Blake, as I feel that is her prerogative.'

'I understand. Thank you. Do you know my birth name? I need to know that, at least.'

'Yes. You were registered as David Carter. Mother, Elisabeth Carter. Father's name withheld. That's all I'm prepared to give you. As I say, your birth mother will give you as much information as she wants you to have.' She paused briefly, then asked, 'How are you feeling now that you know you have a family out there?'

Blake's head was buzzing with the information he had received.

'I'm elated and shocked at the same time,' he admitted. 'Thank you for your help.'

After the call ended, Blake and Caroline sat on the sofa together to discuss his news. After a while, she became quiet.

'What's wrong, dear?' he asked, frowning.

She sighed. 'It's... it's just... well, I think I'm feeling a bit envious that you have a family out there somewhere, and I'm still an unknown mystery.'

He put a protective arm around her, 'You have me, silly. We are family, and no-one can separate us. I don't know how this will pan out. My birth mother might not want to connect, she may have changed her mind, and I'm certainly not going to run off and live with her. Don't worry, pet. We need to get you sorted out when this is settled.'

She smiled. 'I guess I'm over-reacting to your news. Seriously, I'm pleased for you and a bit excited at the thought of you meeting with your family. After all, they will be my in-laws when we marry.'

Blake chuckled. 'Next thing, you will be inviting them to the wedding. Why don't we start the ball rolling to find out who you are? There's no reason to wait any longer. We can contact Hettie for advice. What do you think?'

'Let me sleep on it. It's a massive step to take and I want to be sure I'm ready for it. It was so stressful waiting for your DNA results, I don't know if I can take much more at the moment.'

∞

Lisa Shepley was sitting at home with her daughter, Riley, who was engrossed in her laptop. Her thoughts wandered to the letter she had received from Hettie Moore, indicating that her son had been found and was keen to make contact with her, by whichever means she felt comfortable with.

Looking fondly at her busy daughter, Lisa thought, How will she react to this? She had kept her teenage pregnancy secret from her children until after the death of her husband Lionel. He had been a strict churchgoer and would have been appalled had she revealed her past indiscretion with a boy –, for that was what he was – from her street. Her parents had been horrified and ashamed, and sent her to live with a distant relative until after the baby was born and given up for adoption. Lisa's heart had broken as she held the infant in her arms for the last time before he was gently removed. As she'd hugged him for the final time, she had promised the sleeping babe that someday she would find him. My darling little boy. My David.

Lisa never returned to her home town. She found employment in a hotel that offered accommodation, and some years later, she met and married Lionel Shepley – a kind husband who knew nothing about his wife's background. He believed her story that she had been brought up by an aunt after her parents' death in a car crash. Several years into the marriage and just when she thought they would never have children, two sons Adam and Leo were born within four years of each other. And the arrival of Riley six years later completed the suburban family.

A few weeks after Lionel's death, the family were sifting through paperwork that he had amassed over the years.

'Dad was quite a hoarder, there's stuff going back several years. Why did he hold onto all this?' questioned Adam.

'Oh, you know what he was like,' smiled Lisa wistfully. 'He never threw anything out in case it would come in handy someday.'

Leo shredded another piece of useless paperwork and laughed, 'Hey, wouldn't it be a hoot if we found out our strait-laced father had a skeleton in the cupboard?'

Lisa, flustered and taken aback, jumped and knocked over an ornament that had been on the table. 'Oh, how clumsy of me. I'll fetch a dustpan.'

She almost ran from the room, leaving her children bemused as they looked at each other for answers.

'What's got into Mum?' enquired Riley.

'Something has touched a nerve,' remarked Adam.

When Lisa returned, it was obvious she had been crying.

'Mum, what's wrong? Something has upset you,' said Riley.

Lisa looked at the faces of her young, successful adult children and said, 'Adam, Leo, Riley, I think it's time for me to come clean.'

It was painful for her to admit her teenage indiscretion. Riley moved closer to her mother, held her hands, and said, 'Oh Mum, how awful for you to be treated like that. I often wondered what it would have been like to have grandparents on your side of the family. Gramps was so like Dad, not much fun, and of course we never knew Grandma Shepley.'

Wiping a tear from her eye, Lisa said, 'It was so different in those days. It brought shame on a family to have a child out of wedlock.'

Adam shook his head. 'Mum, you've been brave to keep that secret to yourself all these years. It's no big deal nowadays, but what you must have suffered,' he reassured her with a hug. Leo joined the others and all three hugged their mother and assured her there was no shame to be had.

'Can you understand why I could never tell your father about my baby?' she asked.

Her three children nodded sympathetically. They knew that news of his wife's transgression would not have gone down well with their strict father.

Adam asked, 'Did you ever have any news about your child? Gosh, our brother?'

Lisa shook her head, too emotionally overcome to reply. Eventually, she drew a sharp intake of breath and said, 'Not until a few months ago. I had correspondence from an adoption agency with news that he was searching for me. I couldn't do anything while your father was alive, and now, I'm not sure how I feel. I'm so mixed up.'

'Hey,' smiled Riley. 'I have another brother. Let's hope he's more fun than these two,' she laughed as she teased her elder brothers.

Leo added, 'Mum, can we try to find him? Our brother. That is so cool.'

Lisa was overwhelmed by the positive attitude of her children and, once composed, admitted, 'I would like nothing better than to find my baby. I never stopped thinking about him and always put a prayer up for him on his birthday. He is actually your half-brother, my first-born, my David.'

Adam, always the organiser, said, 'Let's start by you replying to the adoption agency. Do you want to meet him? We certainly do.' He smiled at his siblings and they nodded in agreement.

Lisa fetched the correspondence that she had concealed from her husband, and shared it with her children. When he'd read the letter, Adam said, 'It looks like the guy wants to meet you. Do you feel strong enough to go through with this? Remember, we're right here with you, and we'll support whatever you decide.'

With help from the adoption agency, Lisa wrote an emotional letter to her first-born child, explaining a little of the circumstances of his birth and asking him to get in touch with her. She told him of her other children, his half-siblings, who were keen to meet him. Enclosing her phone number, she sent the letter off to the agency to be forwarded to her son.

It was several weeks before Blake made contact. Although excited at the prospect, he hesitated, fearing a second rejection.

One morning, Lisa answered the telephone, expecting Leo to call, and was taken aback when a man's voice said, 'Hi, I believe you are my mother.'

∞

Julie's dinner party was in full swing. She was an excellent cook and produced wholesome, no-nonsense dishes. Her guests were all in good form – her close friends Liz and Colin, neighbours Jack and Stella Denny, Raymond and Mary Newton, and Liz's nephew Malcolm, who'd had the unenviable experience of discovering the carnage at Safe Haven when the rescue dogs were poisoned some years ago, and found himself wrongly accused of the deed.

As the meal progressed, the conversation came around to a proposed development at Yetts Bank. A developer had applied to build over one hundred houses in a field that had been sold off by the local farmer.

'What on earth possessed Don Bryson to sell off that field?' questioned an angry Jack Denny, who had lived in the village all his life.

'I heard he was nearing retirement and wanted to visit

his daughter in Canada. He must have needed the money,' replied Liz.

Jack continued, 'I spoke to him some months ago when I first heard of his plan to sell the field. I pointed out how it would impact on the village if developers were allowed free reign, but he was adamant about the sale.'

'Can you imagine,' said Liz, swallowing a mouthful of dessert, 'how it will destroy the village as we know it? Once you let one developer in, others will be sure to follow.'

Mary quietly commented, 'As you know, we moved here with our girls a few years ago. We chose Yetts Bank because of its rural setting – a good place to bring up our children, or so we thought. What will happen with the village school? There won't be room for more than a few children.'

Stella Denny chuckled, 'Can you imagine what Jessica Morris will have to say about this? I was in the post office yesterday and she didn't mention it, so the news hasn't reached her yet.'

'That's another problem,' remarked Raymond. 'We will need shops. Our little shop will not cater for all those people.'

Julie laughed. 'I can just see Jessica lining everyone up outside in an orderly queue as she serves her customers. Seriously, though, isn't there anything we can do to stop this development? Jack, have you any thoughts on the matter? We need to do something before the first spade is turned.'

Colin smiled 'Julie, you are our village investigator and sleuth, you should get your teeth into the project to save Yetts Bank.'

Malcolm spoke up. 'We could start by organising a petition. I could help with that. We need to call a public meeting, form a committee, and stop this happening to our village.' The others had never seen the quiet young man so animated. He thumped on the table as he spoke. 'We must stop this.'

'Well said,' replied Colin. Turning to his hostess, he added, 'Julie, are you up for this challenge? We are all behind you.'

'Hmm,' she replied with a mouthful of after dinner mints. 'We certainly need to do something to stop us losing our village status. Yes, let's go for it. Jack, you are on the village hall committee, can you arrange the initial meeting for us? Meanwhile, I'll look into the plans for the development and scrutinise them carefully.'

After coffee and more chat, the visitors headed home, all except Liz and Colin who offered to help tidy up.

'There's no need. I can do that tomorrow,' Julie told them.

'Julie Sinclair, I know you too well. We'll come in here a few days from now and not a dish will have been washed. Anyway,' continued Liz, 'there's still some wine to be finished, so we can kill two birds with one stone while Colin takes the dogs out.'

Before they knew it, the dining room had been cleared, and the dishes washed and put away.

'Where does this go?' asked Liz, as she held a decanter in her hands.

'Just put it on the dresser beside the clock. I'll put it away later.'

'Hey,' remarked Liz, spotting a letter on the dresser. 'Have you done anything about this adoption thing?'

'Oh that. No, I've forgotten about it,' Julie replied dismissively. 'I meant to look into it but, honestly, Liz, do I want to be bothered about finding my origins at my age? Let sleeping dogs lie.'

Liz shrugged. 'If you're not curious, I certainly am. I'm longing for you to find out about your mysterious past. Maggie is, too. We spoke about it just recently.'

Julie laughed. 'Oh, that makes it all worthwhile then. My best buddies requesting me to search for a long-lost mama and papa. Well, I suppose I should do something about it just to satisfy your curiosity.'

Over the next week or two, the village residents rallied around the plan to halt the development of Yetts Bank. Malcolm succeeded in persuading everyone to sign the petition – not that much persuasion was needed – and Jack had arranged a time for a public meeting and invited a representative of Build a Home, the company who had secured the contract. Liz and Mary set about making and distributing posters announcing the event, and Jessica Morris was beside herself with rage at the thought of her treasured post office being overrun with strangers.

'It shouldn't be allowed,' she grumbled as she rose to her full height of not much more than five feet. 'How am I expected to cope with an influx of people wanting to send parcels and goodness knows what else? I'm working all the hours of the day to look after this village. No, I'm not having this invasion. Something has to be done.' She was in her element, making her views known to everyone who crossed the threshold of her beloved premises.

Something was being done. Julie spent several hours studying the plans for development. She came across an old map of the village, showing the field in question, which she discovered had been a former ancient burial ground. 'Eureka!' she called out, much to the excitement of the dogs, who jumped up ready for fun. 'No-one can build on this sacred ground, I'm sure of that.'

She immediately called in next door to share her findings with Jack Denny.

'Jack, have a look at this interesting old map. Look, right here,' she enthused, as she passed the map to him and pointed to the area in question.

'Hmm. I had heard there was a sacred burial place somewhere around this area, but never knew exactly where it was, and I didn't give much thought to it. Good for you, Julie, this might just be what we need to halt development. Can you investigate some more?'

She nodded. 'I intend to find out what I can – not just to stop development, but for historical interest. My first love when I began writing was based on historical events, so this might whet my appetite to take up the theme again.'

Back home, she was searching for paper to make notes about her find, when she came across the letter from her adoptive parents again. *I had better do something about this before Liz and Maggie nag me to death,* she thought with a sigh.

Leaving her village project temporarily on hold, Julie researched how to go about finding her birth parents. When she found an agency that looked promising, she fired off an email enquiring as to how to proceed, not really caring if she heard from them or not.

The night of the public meeting saw the village hall filled to capacity. It was a warm evening, and the windows were open to allow air to circulate in the old building that had seen better days. Everyone, it seemed, had rallied to the cause to save Yetts Bank, and there was a buzz of excitement as the main players took centre stage. Jack Denny, who had been appointed to chair the meeting, began by introducing the panel.

'As residents of Yetts Bank, you all know the people sitting here with me – people you know and trust and whom you have nominated by ballot to serve on this committee. Liz will take minutes and ensure copies are made available to you, either online or in print form. I will give an account of our efforts so far to save our village, then I will invite Mr Williams from Build a Home to speak to us. Feelings are running high, but I ask you to afford our guest the respect he deserves. There will be time for questions later.'

Looking around at the top table, Jack continued, 'One of our committee members, Julie Sinclair – known to you all – appears not to be here yet. Let's hope she will join us before too long. She has a lot to contribute.' He looked quizzically at Liz, but she shrugged her shoulders, having no idea where Julie was.

Stalling for time to allow Julie to arrive with the precious map, Jack went on, 'I am disappointed that our local council representative, James Porter, could not attend, citing a previous commitment.'

There was a hum of discontent in the hall and mutterings of 'typical of him', 'shows no interest in us', 'when did he last show his face here?', we only see him at election time', could be heard.

With no sign of Julie, Jack brought the meeting to order and the discussion began in earnest. Mr Williams was then invited to speak. A portly gentleman whose suit had seen better days, his hair was unkempt, and he did not endear himself to the audience by his condescending manner as he spoke of the advantages of bringing new blood and young families into the area. He droned on, well used to such meetings, and expected his presentation to impress the villagers. He had no interest in what any other speakers had to say; his purpose was to give the facts, answer a few questions, secure a lucrative contract for house building wherever he could, and make money for his floundering company.

Unimpressed, the residents of Yetts Bank did not let him off lightly. They fired question after question at the flustered man, so incensed were they at his lack of empathy with them. Tension rose and voices increased. Jack Denny attempted to keep order, while having every sympathy with his invited guest. Liz – glad to make use of her long-forgotten shorthand skills – wrote furiously, not wanting to miss any comments.

Such was the buzz that no-one had noticed that Julie had entered the hall and was watching proceedings from the back row. As Jack was about to draw the meeting to a halt, he suddenly spotted her. 'I'll take one more question.'

Julie stood up and spoke directly to the now rather flustered and subdued representative of the house builders.

'Mr. Williams, I am sure your company has surveyed the proposed site, am I correct?'

'Of course, my dear. We are very particular about things like that.' He smirked, hoping to dismiss this woman and get out of Yetts Bank.

'Firstly,' replied Julie, 'I am not your dear.' There was a titter of laughter in the hall as she continued. 'In that case, Mr Williams, you will be aware that the field in question is an ancient burial site, and as such, by law, bodies must be respectfully exhumed and reburied elsewhere in sacred ground – a costly exercise to be borne by the developers. I have here all the information you will require to assist your company in the sensitive disinterment. Also, having researched your company, Build A Home, I find it to be in financial difficulties. Can you enlighten us how you propose to pay for the removal of bodies and develop Yetts Bank?'

She walked the length of the hall to hand the information to the bumbling man.

Mr Williams wiped his brow with his handkerchief, his face red with fury and wishing the ground to open up and swallow him.

To prevent any more discomfort for the visitor, Jack Denny quickly brought the meeting to an end, thanked everyone for their attendance, including their guest, and led him swiftly out by the back door. As he did so, there was the sound of applause – not for the unfortunate man, but for Julie. Spontaneous clapping broke out and someone began singing, 'For she's a jolly good fellow.'

Embarrassed by the fuss, she waved her acknowledgement, mouthed her thanks, and left the hall with Liz. Having raced on her bike to the hall, Julie unlocked it and pushed it by her side as she walked back home with her friend.

'Julie saves the day,' Liz said proudly, 'but why were you so late? I was concerned when you hadn't turned up. Jack was almost apoplectic.'

Julie smiled and took an intake of breath before replying. 'I was on my way out when I had a call from a family tracing service. You know I told you I had sent off a DNA sample for matching? Well...'she hesitated before continuing, 'they found a match for my DNA.'

'Go on,' prompted Liz, as she stopped in her tracks.

'I have a sister.'

'Oh, my goodness. Great news...' began Liz.

But Julie was not quite finished. 'Yes, a sister, and there's more. I am an identical twin.'

∞

It was several weeks later when a notice appeared in the local press stating that Build A Home had withdrawn its application to build in Yetts Bank, stating a change in company policy.

∞

Blake sat nervously in a hotel lounge where he had arranged to meet his birth mother. It was a surreal situation to suddenly have a family who wanted to meet him. Several weeks had passed since his first tentative phone call with Lisa Shepley, and they had agreed to take things slowly until they both felt ready to meet face-to-face.

They called each other regularly, and finally agreed a time and place to meet without anyone else around. Time seemed to stand still, and Blake constantly pulled on his jacket sleeve, ran his hand through his hair, and looked at his watch. He was seated in a quiet alcove, away from other hotel guests, and facing the main door of the lounge. He jumped every time it opened, but each time it only revealed a waiter, some guests, or a cleaner.

Eventually the door opened slowly, and a well-dressed lady hesitated as she entered the room. Blake stood.

As their eyes met, he held out both hands to take hers, and said almost in a whisper, 'Hello, Mum.'

Lisa looked at the face of her first-born and felt her emotions surging like a waterfall that she felt unable to control. Tears rolled down her face as her son took her in his outstretched arms and they hugged for a long time. Her body shook uncontrollably as if years of painful pent-up secrecy had been released.

Blake wiped tears from his eyes as they drew apart. He was the first to speak. 'Let's sit down. That must have been a bit of an ordeal for you.'

A waiter appeared and they ordered drinks then sat side by side, holding hands as if never wanting to be parted again. 'We have a lot to catch up on,' Blake went on.

Lisa nodded as she wiped the last of the tears from her face. 'I was dreading that you might reject me and blame me for abandoning you.'

'Never.'

'It was good to talk with you by phone, but now I'm a blubbering woman.'

Blake laughed. 'We broke the ice by calling each other over the past few months. I had a mental picture in my head of what you might look like, you're beautiful.'

Lisa smiled through her tears. 'You're a flatterer,' she responded, but the comment relaxed her.

'Tell me about my half-brothers and sister. What are they like? Do they look like me?' Questions tumbled from his lips as he gazed at the woman beside him.

'Adam is the eldest... well, not now...' she smiled warmly. 'He was the first to be born when I married Lionel Shepley. My husband insisted on naming him Adam; 'the first man,' he said, and my heart missed a beat. I couldn't bring myself to tell him Adam was actually my second son. Anyway, he is thirty-three, in real estate, and doing well. He has a lovely partner, Trudy, and they've been together for four years now. Times have changed when I think of how my pregnancy with you was received. Such shame on the family, so they told me, but I was never ashamed of my baby.'

She stopped to sip her drink before continuing, 'Leo came next, four years after Adam. He is so like you, same facial expressions and sparkling eyes. He is at university doing a Masters in some kind of mathematics that I don't understand. He lives at home with me and Riley. Riley is my only girl. She's a sweet, charming, bubbly young lady, who has just taken up her first teaching post. She's twenty-three and has a boyfriend – a Nigerian student who I have still to meet. She says once she's settled in teaching, she'll bring him home to meet us all.'

Blake smiled wistfully. 'It sounds like you have a lovely family.'

'They want to meet you,' she assured him.' They are keen to get to know their older brother.'

'Same here. I want to meet them, too.'

For the next two hours, mother and son talked as if they had never been apart. Lisa told the little she knew of his biological father. 'He was just a lad from a few doors up, his name was Joe Morton. The family moved away. and I never saw him again.'

Blake told of his own upbringing, firstly with his adoptive parents of whom he had hazy recollections. 'I vaguely remember them. We were sent to live with her sister and her husband who never wanted us there, but felt it their duty to give us a roof over our heads. There was no love for us. We were just tolerated. and both left home as soon as we were old enough.' He sipped his drink before continuing.

'I don't understand...' Lisa interrupted, looking bemused. 'We... us?' she questioned.

'Ah, sorry.' Blake smiled, realising her confusion. 'I should explain. Caroline is my sister... well, she's not my sister... not now. We were brought up as brother and sister and only learned recently that we are not related. We were adopted separately.' He went on to explain about Caroline's change of name, her sad life that saw her end up in prison, and her life now with him.

'We plan to marry once we have sorted out our roots,' he said.

'I would like to meet her.' Lisa wiped away a tear and went on, 'I am sad that you didn't have a happy life. I often wondered and prayed for you, hoping you were doing well at school and were with a loving family. It distresses me now to know you were placed with people who didn't love you.' She looked at her son, dabbed her eyes, and shook her head. 'If I'd known that, I would have searched for you and brought you home, and faced the wrath of my husband.'

Blake took her hands in his, looked into her wet eyes and said, 'It wasn't all that bad. I didn't mean to distress you. Caroline and I were happy together as children, and spent as much time outdoors as we could to get away from the claustrophobic house. Please don't distress yourself. It's all water under the bridge, and has made me a strong person. I had a marvellous time in the Merchant Navy, and they gave me a trade. I'm now a qualified engineer, so life is good.'

He hugged Lisa and said with a smile, 'It sounds like a family reunion is on the cards.'

They talked some more and, when they finally said farewell, he hailed a taxi for his birth mother, planted a kiss on her cheek, and assured her, 'I'll be in touch with a time and place for us all to meet.'

∞

Encouraged by Blake's enthusiasm, Caroline made the decision to follow his lead and start investigating her own birth parents. Hettie Moore once again was called upon to guide the couple through a maze of research.

'The National Records of Scotland, based in Edinburgh, hold all records. After adoption is finalised, the original birth certificate is sealed,' announced Hettie.

That evening, Caroline announced, 'I want to go to Edinburgh and visit the place where records are kept. Shirley, you remember her, she was my cell mate. We've kept in touch. She's coming to Edinburgh for the Festival, and suggests we meet up. I'd like to meet her again; she helped me survive prison.'

Blake frowned. 'I'm not sure that's a good idea. By all means meet with your friend, but leave the search for your birth parents to the experts. I want to be with you if you get a result in case, it's negative. We can do the searching together and Hettie will guide us. Please don't go dabbling in it without me. I don't want you to be hurt.'

Caroline shrugged. 'I'll think about it, but I really do want to meet Shirley.'

He knew how headstrong she could be, and hoped she wouldn't do anything silly like taking off on her own to meet her friend. But one evening a few weeks later, he arrived home from work to find the house deserted and a note propped up where he would see it:

Gone to Edinburgh for a few days, meeting Shirley, taking in a show, and while I'm there, I'll arrange a visit to the records office. Sorry for short notice, but it's the only free time that Shirley has. I'll call you. Love, C x

Blake was furious. The last thing he wanted was for her to react badly to a negative result, as she was still vulnerable when not with him. The weekend was looming, and he decided to head for Edinburgh to find her. Her actions both frustrated and saddened him.

∞

With his search for his fiancée well and truly over and, with an anger he never knew he possessed, he returned home to the cold apartment. The chill came more from the coldness he felt at that moment for Caroline. He slept fitfully that night, his mind in a turmoil. Why did she ignore me? Is this her subtle way of telling we are finished as a couple? Do I truly know this person?

With these thoughts tumbling around his head, he eventually slept, and woke late in the day to the clatter of dishes. Caroline had returned.

'So, you've come home?' snapped Blake, as he stood at the entrance to the kitchen watching her setting.

At the sound of his voice, she turned, smiled, and was about to throw her arms around him when she noticed his demeanour. She had never seen him angry like this – not even in the dark days when they lived with the Broadbents.

'Hi, darling. I didn't want to wake you. You were in a deep sleep.'

Blake did not move from the spot.

'Darling, what's wrong?' Caroline felt a fear rush through her body. This was so unlike him.

'If you want to end our relationship, say so now.'

'What? Blake, you're frightening me. What are you talking about? Of course, I don't want to end it, what's got into you? Have you been dreaming?'

His expression was cold, his voice harsh. 'No, not dreaming, but maybe I've had the wool pulled over my eyes. Am I only a meal ticket for you? Don't you have any real feelings for me?'

Caroline was beginning to panic. Was he ill? Had he succumbed to some kind of strange illness? She'd seen that kind of delusionary behaviour when living in the squat. Surely he hadn't been using drugs?

'Blake, I'm scared. I've never seen you like this. What's wrong, darling? Everything is fine between us.'

'Everything is fine?' he shouted. 'Then explain your crass behaviour in Edinburgh. Why did you ignore me? Were you ashamed of me meeting your posh pals?'

Caroline looked mystified. 'I didn't ignore you. I never saw you in Edinburgh. I didn't know you were in the capital. And what posh friends? I was with Shirley; I told you I was meeting her.'

'So, you weren't at the evening performance at the theatre?' he snapped back. 'You weren't in the lounge of the Festival Hotel? Come on, I'm not taking this nonsense. I saw you with my own eyes.'

Caroline could take no more of this confusion and burst into tears.

'Ah, tears of remorse?'

She rushed from the kitchen and curled up into a foetal position on the sofa, totally confused and scared.

Blake went for a shower. He let the water run over him, tears running down his face. What is happening to us?

When he was dried and dressed, he emerged from the bedroom calmer and ready to have a serious talk. Caroline was still curled up on the sofa, her eyes red from crying.

He sat down beside her and said quietly, 'We need to sort this out.'

'Blake, I really don't know what you're talking about. Yes, I was in Edinburgh. Okay, I know you're mad at me for taking off without telling you, but Shirley called to say her days off had been changed at the last minute. I couldn't contact you at work, because you told me never to do that as personal calls are frowned upon. I was with Shirley and no-one else. We didn't stay or go into that hotel; I don't even know where it is. We just about scraped enough money between us for a guest house in Leith, and that's where we spent the day, visiting the Royal Yacht Britannia that's berthed there, and looking at the shops at the Ocean Terminal.' A sudden thought struck her, and she jumped up to fetch her handbag. 'Look... here is the receipt for it and the receipt for the guest house. Yes, we went to the theatre, but to an afternoon performance; here's my ticket stub. When we found out the National Records place was shut, we decided to get out of Edinburgh, it's too crowded and Shirley is claustrophobic after being banged up in prison. We took the bus. Here's my ticket.'

Blake had often teased her about the number of things she had in her bag, but Caroline was glad she'd kept all her receipts now. She waited quietly as he perused the various bits of paper then handed them back.

He looked into her eyes and saw hurt and fear. Immediately, he felt guilty. Was he so capable of frightening the woman he loved?

They were both silent for a time before Blake spoke. 'I'm sorry to have doubted you, but I had a very weird experience. When I got your note about going to Edinburgh, I admit I was angry. I didn't want you to discover anything about your birth mother without my being by your side, so I headed there. I should have realised that looking for you would be a thankless task in those crowds, but... Caroline... darling, this is the strange thing...'

He paused for breath, looked straight at her, then continued, 'I saw you coming out of the theatre in the evening with three friends. I called out but you ignored me. I was hurt and angry, thinking you were ashamed to be seen with me, as your friends looked well-to-do. I discreetly followed you to a very upmarket hotel and wondered how on earth you could afford to stay there. When I spotted you on your own in the lounge, I tried to speak to you, but again you ignored me. I'm ashamed to say I caused a bit of a fuss and was asked to leave the premises. Caroline, I would swear on the Bible that I saw you, but obviously it wasn't you. Now, I feel such a fool. You must have a double. It's uncanny.'

They hugged for a long time, each sobbing quietly with relief. All was well again with the couple.

∞

Sometime after meeting his birth mother, a family get-together was arranged in the same hotel where they had first met. On a bright Spring day, Blake and Caroline arrived, ready to meet his family.

'I'm excited for you. Who will all be there?' she asked.

'I'm not sure. Lisa texted to confirm the arrangements and said she hoped all her children would manage along, as they were anxious to meet us both.'

As they entered the lounge area, they were drawn to a crowd chatting excitedly. Lisa spotted them and stood to greet her first-born and his fiancée.

Blake spoke. 'I've been so looking forward to this day. This is Caroline, my fiancée. Caroline darling, this is Lisa, my... mother.' He said the word almost reverently.

The three hugged and were soon surrounded by several other people. Lisa composed herself and introduced her newly-found son to his siblings.

'Blake, my David... this is Adam, and Leo, your brothers. And last but not least, your sister Riley.'

It was a surreal few minutes for them all, as they shook hands and hugged each other. Riley, especially, was over-excited as she hugged both Blake and Caroline.

'I couldn't sleep last night,' she babbled, 'for thinking about you both and wondering what you looked like.'

The next few hours passed too quickly before Adam and Leo announced they had to leave for appointments.

'It's been great meeting our elder brother,' said Leo.

'We'll keep in touch,' added Adam, as he backslapped his new brother in a male bonding gesture.

Blake and his mother sat together holding hands and talking quietly as Riley and Caroline chatted non-stop, comparing likes and dislikes, books, work, films, and fashion.

'Riley is a chatterbox,' smiled her mother. 'Caroline will have a hard time trying to get a word in, but the girls seem to have clicked. Your fiancée is a wonderful young woman and I wish you both every happiness together.'

The group parted company to take up the threads of life but with an exciting new addition. A family.

∞

Some weeks later, Caroline asked Blake for change of twenty pounds.

'In my wallet, dear,' he called from the spare room they had converted to an office.

As Caroline swapped her note for smaller denominations, a business card fell out of the wallet. She looked at it, turned it around, and called through to Blake, 'Who is Julie Sinclair? Have you a secret admirer?' She laughed as she took the card through to him.

Without looking up from his computer, he replied, 'Never heard of her. Who is she, anyway?'

'Here, look at it.'

'Ah, I remember,' he said. 'I saw her in Edinburgh and thought she was you. The similarity was amazing. That's who I saw. I feel so embarrassed when I think back to that evening.' He studied the card, turning it over in his hands.

'The hotel manager told me she was a well-known author. Let's Google her and check her out.'

He keyed in the details from the card and waited. 'Well, her books look interesting. Here, have a look.' He moved over to allow Caroline a better view, and they scrolled down to some pictures of a book event.

Caroline frowned as she studied the pictures rather than the selection of books. 'Hey, is someone impersonating me? Using my picture to promote themselves? This is weird. Wait. I never had a sweater that colour. Have these pictures been doctored? Blake, I don't understand.'

There was silence for a minute, then Blake whispered, 'I think I do.'

They perused the site for some time to learn as much as they could about the mysterious woman who looked so like Caroline.

'I'm going to email her,' Blake said eventually. 'I owe her an apology for startling her, and I'll explain how alike she is to you. Let's do it and see what transpires.' He turned to kiss his fiancée. 'Darling, I'm sorry for doubting you.'

Caroline threw her arms around him. 'That's all water under the bridge,' she said with a smile. 'Let's find out who the heck this Julie woman is and why she has my face.'

∞

Julie hesitated before opening the email from an unknown source, and stared at the sender's name: Blake Jessop. Where have I come across that name before? she wondered. She was used to receiving letters from readers commenting on her work, in fact she encouraged such correspondence, but was always careful to avoid being hacked. Unable to contain her curiosity, she opened the email.

Please allow me to apologise unreservedly for my behaviour towards you some months ago when I rudely approached you in Edinburgh in the street, and later in the hotel where you were staying. You must have thought I was some kind of madman. I can now explain the cause of my erratic behaviour. My fiancée, Caroline, was in Edinburgh at that time and I was frantic to find her. The resemblance between you is remarkable and I genuinely mistook you for her.

I have enclosed an attachment showing a recent picture of her, and I am sure you will agree that you look very much alike. I was given your business card by the manager of the hotel when he, figuratively speaking, kicked me out into the street, but I just came across it this week.

Ms Sinclair, accept my genuine apology, and if there is anything I can do to atone for my behaviour, please let me know. Perhaps you have a favourite charity that I could donate to.

Yours humbly,

Blake Jessop

Immediately, Julie remembered where she had come across that name, and went to look in the pocket of the jacket she had worn on her weekend break. Seeing her reach for her jacket, the dogs jumped about excitedly, hoping that a walk was imminent.

After rummaging in the pockets, she pulled out a card. Ah yes, Blake Jessop. I remember you. She went back to her computer and clicked on the email attachment, but gasped as she found herself staring at her double. Oh, my goodness, no wonder he was confused. This is uncanny. She re-read the message and studied the picture in front of her for a considerable time before forwarding the email to Liz and Maggie with a comment: This explains it.

Her friends lost no time in setting up a Zoom chat.

Liz, barely able to contain her excitement, said, 'Didn't I say you had a doubleganger?'

Maggie chipped in cheerfully, 'Well, that certainly does explain things. He wasn't a madman out to seduce or murder you, after all. What are you going to do about the email? Will you reply?'

'Oh, you must,' insisted Liz, as she petted one of her dogs who had climbed onto her lap. 'This is the best non-fiction story you've ever been involved in.'

'I'll give it serious thought,' Julie replied. 'This could be important. I'll mull things over before I reply, out of politeness if not curiosity. Yes, girls, I'll contact my stalker.'

She waited a few days before firing off a reply to Blake, stating how relieved she was to have an explanation for the strange encounter in Edinburgh and accepting his apology, before continuing: 'My friend flippantly suggested I must have a doubleganger, and strangely enough I recently researched my past as I was adopted at birth, and have discovered that I have a sister. Is this a coincidence? Your fiancée certainly has a marked resemblance to me. Perhaps we are distantly related.'

Blake called for Caroline to read the email that had popped up in his inbox.

'Honey, read this.'

Caroline, her arms around his shoulders, read and re-read the correspondence from the woman who looked so like her. 'Blake. What does this mean? Is this woman related to me?'

'I don't know, darling, but it is uncanny. I think it's time for us to contact Hettie Moore and research your past. Are you up for it?'

'Yes. This has spurred me on to do something about finding my origins. This Julie person may be distantly related.

Let's investigate. But shouldn't we ask her permission to share this email with Hettie?'

'Oh course, I should have thought of that. Yes, that would be the polite thing to do. I'll reply immediately.'

Julie wasted no time in giving her consent.

Hettie, with the forwarded email and pictures of both Julie and Caroline, was excited at the challenge in front of her. A quick call to the latter to request she take a DNA test similar to Blake's, set in motion a string of events that was to impact on several lives.

Time seemed to go slowly as the couple waited for the result of the DNA, watching anxiously for mail to pop through their letterbox. Each time they heard a letter drop onto the mat, they rushed to retrieve it. 'Oh dash, just circulars and adverts.' Caroline had bitten her nails down to the quick, her anxiety levels were so high.

Blake insisted she take a day off from work to rest.

'You'll make yourself ill if you don't calm down. The result will come when it comes.' He was anxious about her state of mind and how she would react if the result was negative. Perhaps on hindsight, I should have left well alone and not insisted we follow up that email. We could be on a wild goose chase.

A few weeks later, Hettie called to say she had made progress. 'I have to double check some information before I pass my findings on to you. I want to be absolutely sure of the result, but it looks like there is a match to Caroline's DNA. I promise to be in touch as soon as I have verified my findings.'

The next few days were tense as they waited for information. Finally, long-awaited correspondence arrived, and Caroline's hands shook as she attempted to open the envelope. 'You open it for me, I'm shaking.'

Blake carefully extracted the enclosed paperwork that they spread out on the table to reveal that Caroline had a living relative. 'Here's a copy of my birth certificate! Oh, Blake, I'm so nervous.' With his arm around her shoulders she read, 'Gabrielle Coogan, second of twin daughters born to mother, Orla Coogan, and father William Hanrahan, both of Galway, Eire.'

Her date of birth was as she thought, but her place of birth was given as a mother and baby unit in Scotland.

'Gabrielle,' teased Blake, 'that's rather a posh name for you. Hey, I like it.'

Caroline, stunned as she took in the implication of her findings, faltered as she said, 'I'm Irish. Looks like my birth parents never married. Oh Blake, I'm so excited. I have a twin; a living relative that we need to track down.'

Blake thought about the picture of Julie Sinclair and mused, 'Mm, I wonder if she has Irish connections? Let's contact her and ask. I'm sure she won't mind the intrusion.'

'Should we forward the results to her?' questioned Caroline, still gripping the letter from Hettie.

'No, let's wait until we hear back from her,' Blake replied. 'We don't really know this woman.'

Blake had given little indication in his email as to the reason for his enquiry, but Julie, naturally inquisitive, wanted to know more. She replied that her parents were Irish, from Galway, but that she herself was born in Scotland. She chose not to divulge any more details of her life until she heard back from Blake.

She did not have long to wait. An email with an attachment landed in her inbox. The attachment stunned her as she read aloud, Gabrielle, twin daughter of Orla Coogan... Oh goodness, the same mother, same date of birth, same place of birth, same father.

She removed her glasses, sat back in her chair, and chewed the end of her pen as she took in the full extent of what she had read. She knew she had found another part of her puzzled life. I need fresh air.

Never known to refuse a walk, two excited dogs joined her as they headed out through the village to Safe Haven. As they passed by the post office, Jessica Morris – always able to hear if a potential customer was approaching from miles away – popped her head out of the door when she realised that Julie was walking by.

'Cooee, Julie. You seem to be in a world of your own. Is everything alright with you? Is there anything I can help with?'

Startled at her thoughts being interrupted, Julie replied, 'Everything is fine, Jessica. Just fine.' She walked on quickly to avoid being waylaid.

Watching her carefully, Jessica shook her head and thought, Things aren't just fine with her, I'm sure something is going on. What could it be?

Liz was working in the dog's paddock and heard Julie's dogs approach before she spotted their owner.

'Those animals have an inbuilt radar, they know where they are when they arrive at the gate,' she told Julie, who released the dogs to greet Liz with their usual exuberance. They knew that treats were to be found in the large pockets of her dress, and were not disappointed.

'This is an unexpected pleasure and calls for a glass or two,' Liz went on. 'Let's go inside. The gate is closed, the dogs are safe.'

The two friends sat in the messy sitting room, Julie slumped into a well-worn armchair, while Liz sat on the floor and poured out wine.

'So, what brings you here – not that I'm not delighted to see you – and with such a thoughtful face?'

'Have a read at this,' she handed over Blake's email which she'd printed off, along with the attachment from Caroline, and waited for a response.

Bemused, Liz looked up from the correspondence at her friend's face. 'This is unbelievable. You know what this means? You not only have a living relative, but you have a sister, an identical twin as you knew from your recent findings and she is... Gosh, the Caroline from Edinburgh! This document is confirmation. How weird is that?'

Julie nodded. 'I've been deep in thought since this popped into my inbox. It is surreal and certainly confirms that Blake Jessop genuinely thought I was his fiancée. So, there we have it. I have a sibling.' She took a gulp of her wine, and added quietly, 'Do I really want a sibling?'

'Oh, let's call Maggie, she needs to know the latest news. Oh, course you want a sister. You used to long for one when we were at school. Remember? You fantasised about it.'

'Liz, dear, have you forgotten that Mags is in California at Robin's wedding, and won't be home until next week.'

Liz sighed. 'Of course. I had forgotten. Your news has taken me by surprise, and I can't think straight. No, we don't want to interrupt the festivities. Let's Zoom her at home next week. She will want to tell us all about the wedding, and we can tell the tale of your Edinburgh stalker. I can't get over this. It calls for a toast to the mysterious Caroline.'

As predicted, on her return from California, Maggie wasted no time in contacting her friends to regale them with news of her son's nuptials. She hardly drew breath as she told every minute detail of the event.

'And what a wonderful surprise we had. Robin had kept secret the fact that Hermione, Jonny's sister, had flown over from Australia. We had such a great time catching up with everyone. And as for Amy-Lee, she was a beautiful bride, such a sweet person, and so suited to my darling son. I have lots of pictures to show you. I'll upload them as soon as I've recovered from the excitement. Robin has promised to bring his wife to visit us at Chestermere Hall.

'Amy-Lee's parents were the nicest people ever, Eddie and Laura,' Maggie chattered on, 'they were so proud of their daughter and just adore my Robin, but then who wouldn't love Robin? Now, Liz, Julie, what have you two been up to during my travels? Anything happening with you, or has life carried on at a sedate pace?'

Liz laughed. 'Us? Sedate pace? Wait until you hear what's developed in our very own Julie's life.'

'Oh, do tell.'

Before Julie had a chance to reply, Liz, eager to share the news, continued, 'She's only gone and found her identical twin.'

There was a brief silence, then Maggie replied, 'What! Do tell all.'

'And,' an excited Liz went on, 'she has solved the mystery of the Edinburgh stalker.'

'Oh, come on, release me from my curiosity.'

At last, Julie was free to speak, and she laughed at Liz's enthusiasm and Maggie's inquisitiveness. 'It started with the e-mail I shared with you from Blake Jessop, who apologised for upsetting me. Remember?'

'Yes,' Maggie remembered. 'That was just before I left for Robin's wedding and you were unsure of whether to reply or not.'

'I did reply and so much has happened since then.' Julie went on to update Maggie on events, with Liz cheerily interrupting.

'Maggie, I'm trying to persuade our dithering friend to follow this up and meet her twin.'

'Oh, course you must. Julie, you really must meet her and visit beautiful Ireland and find your origins. Do it, my dear. You can't let things go unfinished. I'm thrilled for you, even if you are the most unenthusiastic person among us. You know Liz and I will hound you until you meet this woman.'

'Do I really need this in my life at this stage?' Julie argued with them. 'I've gone all these years without a sister. Do I want one encroaching on my privacy?'

'Oh Julie, you are insufferable,' exclaimed Maggie. 'You've come this far, so get on with it, girl. We want to see pictures of you and your twin. It should be exciting, but you are making it out to be worse than a visit to the dentist.'

Liz added, 'Go, explore your Irishness. It will be a great adventure for you both to find your roots. Galway looks beautiful. I've checked it out. Do go.'

Julie's friends were exasperated at her reluctance to discover her birth story. But she was comfortable with who she was, enjoyed her own company, and was particular about choosing friends.

'At least think of it from your sister's side,' Maggie pleaded with her. 'She obviously has a need to follow this through, so go ahead, meet her, say "hello", and take it from there. Even if you return home in the same frame of mind, you will have assisted someone in their quest and, Julie, you always want to help people.'

'Hmm... well, I suppose I should follow it up.'

∞

Some months later, Julie sat in the lounge of a Dublin hotel where she had arranged to meet Caroline. She had hesitated about proceeding with the meeting and, without encouragement from Liz and Maggie, she would have called it off.

Reluctantly, she had purchased a ticket for the sail to Dublin. 'I'm taking my car, so I'll have a get-out if I find it all too suffocating.'

Caroline, on a flight to Dublin, looked out of the window as the aircraft approached its destination. She had not slept for several nights, tossing and turning, disturbing Blake to the point that he had retired to the spare room.

As she neared what she hoped would be the end of her search for answers to her beginnings in life, she was filled with a mixture of excitement and trepidation. Have I done the right thing? What if this woman rejects me?

The sisters had communicated by email for several months, and Caroline had downloaded some of Julie's books. At least we can discuss her writing, she mused, as she read through the emails, attempting to build a picture in her mind of what kind of person she was about to meet. She read and re-read Julie's website and studied her pictures, never failing to be stunned at the resemblance to herself.

Julie was less enthusiastic on hearing the lifestyle of her sibling. Concerned about her time in prison, her drug abuse, and rather disturbing lifestyle, she wondered what kind of person she was going to meet.

But Maggie was quick to reprimand her. 'Julie, it's not like you to judge people; you are the least judgemental person I know. What's got into you?'

'Oh, Mags, I expect it's the whole adoption thing. I wish I'd never let you folks talk me into this. Maybe I've just stirred up a hornet's nest.'

'I understand that it must be stressful and it's taking you out of your comfort zone,' her friend assured her. 'Think of it as a great adventure and, who knows, you might even enjoy it if you can lift that dark cloud of doubt from your mind.'

'Maggie, you are right as usual. I admit to being apprehensive... me, the unflappable Julie Sinclair, who never lets anything faze her, scared to death.'

∞

The hotel was crowded, but Julie managed to find a seat facing the lounge door. She was tempted to order another glass of wine but thought the better of it. I need a clear mind for this, she thought, as she toyed with the wine glass, twirling it around her fingers as she jumped each time the door opened. She had dressed informally in neat denims and a blue coloured top. A cardigan casually draped around her shoulders completed her attire.

Finally, the door opened to reveal a tall, striking woman dressed in a blue trouser suit, with a scarf draped around her shoulders. The two looked at each other. It seemed a long time before either spoke. Julie stood to greet the woman who looked identical to her. It was like looking in a mirror, she later told her friends.

'Hi, I'm Julie and you no doubt are Caroline.'

Caroline smiled as the two hugged cautiously. 'Gosh. I didn't expect you to be so like me... this is eerie.'

A waiter appeared with a lunch menu which they perused before ordering, giving them time to draw breath. They laughed as they both ordered omelette with salad.

'Seems we have the same culinary tastes,' smiled Julie, as she studied the face of her newly found sister. It was surreal. She felt nervous. Part of her wanted to flee from the situation, but her inquisitive nature rejected the idea.

Caroline, always cautious about forming relationships with anyone, studied the woman sitting opposite. She felt anxious. The meal arrived, giving them an excuse to concentrate on everything other than what really mattered. As they chatted politely, though, nerves subsided, and they relaxed as they exchanged life stories. Julie was surprised at how comfortable she felt as she listened to the rather sad upbringing that her sibling had endured, compared to her own more contented and privileged life.

They compared likes and dislikes and giggled as they found several similar traits.

'I hate marmite, too.'

'I can't stand spinach, either.'

'My favourite colour is blue.'

They spoke of their tastes in films and discover they both enjoyed thrillers.

'Unfortunately, due to my own fault in dogging off from school, my reading skills were never up to much,' Caroline smiled. 'And now I have the incentive I need to read more. Which of your books should I start with?'

After discussing Julie's writing, talk moved on to pets.

'Hey, I love dogs, too, although I've never had one of my own,' enthused Caroline. 'Tell me about yours.' She was horrified to hear of the tragedy that had befallen Julie's pets at the hands of a poisoner, and was engrossed in Scamper's role in helping solve a transatlantic crime.

'What an adventure you've had with your animals. Blake would love to have a dog, but until we have a place with a garden, he won't consider it.'

As time moved on, the sisters forgot their initial inhibitions and felt more at ease in each other's presence. Two hours had passed since they first met, and neither woman was anxious for their time together to end. Caroline spoke openly of her dark days of drugs and prison.

'Honestly, prison was the saving of me. I fully expected a fine or community service, but to be banged up for twelve months... well... I tell you, it shook me rigid. There were so many broken lives in there, but I was fortunate to share a cell with two women who set me on the right path. In fact, Shirley keeps in touch, and met me in Edinburgh at the time of Blake's encounter with you. How scary that must have been for you, and how confusing for poor Blake. He thought I'd lost my mind by ignoring him. Actually,' she admitted, 'it almost ended our relationship.'

Julie smiled as she recalled the event. 'We can laugh at it now, but at the time I thought he was some kind of madman. Now I know why the guy in the theatre who showed us to our seats commented, "You must have really enjoyed the show this afternoon if you've come back for a second time." Poor guy. I smiled and said nothing, because I hadn't a clue what he meant. I do hope I get to meet your Blake properly. I've enjoyed our email conversations.'

'Boy, won't that be hilarious if we are together as he tries to figure out who's who?'

'Yes, especially if we arrange to wear the similar outfits.'

They laughed until the tears rolled down their cheeks.

Discovering that they had the same taste in wine, they ordered a bottle and enjoyed several more hours together before Julie, the practical one, reminded her sister that they had a long day ahead of them.

'I'm excited at the prospect of visiting our family estate,' commented Caroline, as she sipped the last of her wine. 'Imagine me being from the landed gentry.'

Julie added, 'And I guess that was the problem. I'm expecting to find that our birth mother was pregnant with us out of wedlock – such an old-fashioned notion nowadays – and brought disgrace on the household. That's my view on it.'

'Yes, mine, too. We were probably an embarrassment to the family and had to be got rid of. Gosh, aren't we lucky she didn't abort us?'

'We have a long drive ahead of us, right out into the country,' Julie said. 'The case worker who helped me find you discovered that the estate was sold off to pay debts some years ago and is now an upmarket spa resort. She knew nothing of the whereabouts of any family or staff, so we're going into this with little or no information.'

'Maybe they will give us a free spa session,' chuckled Caroline, 'especially if we reveal who we are. I hope someone there will give us an idea of what happened to the family.'

The women called it a night and retired to their respective rooms. Caroline immediately contacted Blake to tell of her encounter with her twin. Julie, unable to sleep, paced the room, mulling over the encounter with her double.

∞

The following day began with hazy sunshine, a heat haze that lifted during the course of the day to shed its warmth over the area. Both women laughed as they met for breakfast, dressed in almost similar denims and tops, causing whispered comments from the other guests.

'Snap', exclaimed Caroline.

'Snap,' laughed Julie.

As they drove into the country, remarking on the spectacular scenery as they went, they chatted as if they had known each other all their lives, totally in tune with each other. Julie elicited more from Caroline about her difficult upbringing, and felt guilty at the memory of judging the woman until a reprimand from Maggie had brought her to her senses. Caroline's tale was harrowing.

'I left school at sixteen and ran away from home. I hitched a lift with a lorry driver, who took me with him to Liverpool and dropped me off in the middle of the city. I was never so scared in all my life. I slept in a shop doorway until a Salvation Army lady found me and took me to a homeless shelter, where I stayed for a few weeks until they found me a place in a hostel. I got in with bad company and spiralled downwards from thereon in. In a way, going to prison was a life-saving move for me.'

When they stopped for a coffee break in a picturesque village not far from their destination, Caroline spotted a leaflet advertising Harmony Meadow Spa Resort.

'Wow, Julie, look at this house and grounds. Stunning.'

The two pored over the leaflet, looking at the various interior scenes. 'I can't wait to get there and see our family seat in reality,' continued the excited Caroline. 'I wish we could claim it as ours.'

Julie smiled. 'Well, we know I was first born, older by thirty minutes, so any claim is mine first and foremost.'

Caroline laughed, then became serious. 'How do you like your birth name? Kathleen. Kathleen Coogan, or perhaps, Hanrahan.'

'It doesn't seem like me. I'm Julie, always Julie. What about you? Gabrielle. Do you feel comfortable with the name?'

'I'm not at all sure it fits with my lifestyle,' she laughed. 'It seems too posh a name for an ex-con.'

'You would suit the shorter version, Gabby. What do you think?'

'Hmm, not sure. Gabby Speirs, or Gabby Coogan, or Gabby Hanrahan. Oh, it is so confusing. Here I am trying to find my roots and getting myself muddle-headed with such a variety of names. Who the heck am I?'

Julie laughed at the frustrated woman whose brows were creased as she pondered her name, 'For the moment, you are you, and always will be. A change of name won't alter who you are.'

Caroline smiled and nodded in agreement, as if deferring to her sister.

They drove on into bright sunlight, their spirits cheerful as they anticipated what the day ahead might offer.

'There's the sign, Julie, we almost missed it, on the right down this road.'

About a mile on, they caught their first glimpse of the house that they believed was their ancestral home if the information they had been given was correct.

'Wow. What a pad.'

They drove slowly along the path that brought the house into view, and took in every detail of the stunning grounds that were neatly tended and landscaped. Spring flowers bordered the path and exhibited a welcoming sight in the mild breeze, as if inviting visitors to proceed.

'What are we going to say?' asked Caroline, agog at the beauty of the place. 'We can't just charge in and say, hey, this is our home. Oh, I'm shivering, and I'm scared.'

Julie, becoming used to Caroline's ways and warming to her as a person, smiled and said, 'I'm older and wiser than you, little sister, so leave it to me.'

They parked the car and took in the magnificence of the building before climbing a curved stairway to the front door. A notice invited visitors to ring the bell and enter the foyer. The bell tinkled and drew the attention of the young receptionist who was busy on a computer. She looked in astonishment as two identical women approached.

'Oh. Can I help you? Sorry to stare, but I've never seen people so alike as you are. Forgive me.' She spoke with a

European accent that they were later to learn was Polish. Her name tag showed her name as Krysia. 'Do you have a reservation?'

Julie took charge of the conversation, leaving Caroline dumbstruck as she looked around the foyer.

'No, we don't plan to stay, at the moment. We were in the area and would like to see around the place if that is possible. We believe that relatives of ours were previous owners. This is our first visit.'

'We like to show guests what we offer in this stunning building. I'll call for my colleague, Marysia, to show you around.'

She spoke into her radio receiver, and before long a young smiling assistant arrived to show them around. She was obviously used to conducting such tours, and spoke enthusiastically of the various treatments on offer, believing the women to be potential customers. Julie and Caroline were silent as she enthused about Harmony Meadows. As they moved from one area to another, they were in awe at the décor, the high ceilings, and the stained-glass windows above the staircase, while attempting to listen to Marysia. Julie was particularly enthralled when shown the library, and longed to stay and peruse the books.

After a whirlwind tour, their guide offered them some refreshments in the quiet lounge and left them to mull over some brochures.

'Gosh,' whispered Caroline, feeling the need to keep her voice down as she stretched her neck to observe the ornate ceiling. 'This place is beyond anything I expected. Can you imagine what it would have been like to have been brought up here? What have we missed?'

As they sat relaxing in the beautiful room, Krysia the receptionist joined them.

'Excuse me for interrupting. Steve, our watchman, happened to be in the building collecting his phone that he mislaid, and I mentioned to him that you believe relatives of yours once lived here.'

'Yes,' replied Julie, as she set the fine china teacup down, 'we do believe so.'

'Steve is in his eighties. He should have retired many years go, but insists on being around the place while he is capable of being our security man. He would like to meet you, if you don't mind.'

The women looked at each other before Julie nodded and replied, 'That would be very nice. Thank you, Krysia.'

A few minutes later, a sprightly gentleman arrived. Weather-beaten from years of outdoor work, he held himself erect and proud, and stared as he looked at the visitors.

'Krysia tells me you think relatives of yours lived here. Excuse me staring, you are so... so alike, but not only that...' he hesitated. 'Begorrah. I think I know who you are.'

'You do?' questioned Julie, smiling in the hope of putting the gentleman at ease. 'But?' she questioned with her eyes.

'I hesitated, ma'am, because it's taken me breath away. You are so like the lovely colleen Orla, who was the daughter of the Coogan family who lived here when I began as a gardener's apprentice.'

Caroline could hardly contain her excitement as she invited Steve to sit with them. 'Please, what can you tell us about the family?

Steve scratched his head as if recalling memories of times gone by.

'Well, ma'am,' he began, 'as I say, I came here as a lad of fourteen years. Folks around here didn't hold much with schooling and such like, and most of the lads and colleens were keen to start work. I remember the family well. The head of the house was scary to me as a new boy; a very tall gentleman who lorded it over the household. His wife was kind and used to give me food when no-one was looking. A grand lady she were, grand indeed. There were two sons, Gerald and Anthony, and a daughter, Orla. She was a real beauty; all the boys around here were in love with her. I never knew what happened to her; she was here one day and gone the next. The story was that she'd gone to some posh school abroad. Switzerland or France, or somewhere foreign. Sure, and here I am, an old fool telling you what's mixed up in my memory, and the person you really want to talk to is Amelia O'Riordan, who was the nanny to the family, and their governess. As far I know, she accompanied the young colleen abroad. Amelia lives not far from here in a village about ten miles south. Like me, she's getting on in years, but she has all her buttons, if you know what I mean. A grand woman if ever there was. Would you like me to phone her?'

'Please, that would be kind of you. We would like to meet her.' Caroline was becoming more confident in taking the lead.

Steve returned with a piece of paper that he handed to Caroline. 'That's Amelia's details, and she would be happy to meet you any time after three o'clock. A grand woman, so she is.'

After Steve left, the women thanked Krysia and left with an armful of leaflets and a spring in their step.

∞

They drove along in silence, with Julie concentrating on manoeuvring through country roads that were never intended for anything more than farm vehicles, while Caroline looked out for their destination.

'I have butterflies in my stomach at the thought of getting nearer to finding out about our past,' said Caroline.

'I've been like that since the moment I set eyes on you, and you turned my world upside down with your enthusiasm.'

'Here we are on the outskirts of the village. Steve said to drive as far as the post office and take a right.'

At the mention of post office, Julie's mind momentarily turned to Jessica Morris and how she would react to this adventure. She would milk every last detail from Julie.

'Oh, what a pretty little house, Irish Heatherlie Cottage. Are we ready for this, Caroline?'

'Let's go. We've come this far. Hey, you go first.'

Julie smiled, 'Are you giving me my place as eldest sister or are you nervous?'

'Oh, go on. Ring that bell before my heart bursts with excitement.'

They waited a few minutes before a frail voice called out, 'The door is unlocked, please come in. Sure, and we never lock our doors in Ireland.'

Amelia O'Riordan's life seemed to stand still as she looked at the two women who had entered her little home. She was speechless as she showed them into her cosy sitting room. She hadn't spoken a word, so shocked was she at seeing them.

Julie, aware of how the woman stared, said, 'Thank you for taking the time to see us. I hope we're not disturbing you.'

Amelia shook her head and somehow found her voice. 'Oh, my dears, forgive an old lady's rudeness in staring. Please sit by me. Sure, now, and you're not disturbing me.'

Caroline began by introducing herself. 'I am Caroline Speirs, and this is Julie Sinclair. We believe you can tell us something of the family who lived in what is now Harmony Meadows Spa Resort. We are trying to find our origins, and research has led us here.'

Julie produced some paperwork that she handed to Amelia, who donned her reading glasses and read their contents. She folded the papers, handed them back to Julie, removed her glasses, smiled, and looked at the two as they awaited her response.

'Sure, now, and I don't need any paperwork to tell me who you are. As soon as I saw you two beautiful angels, I knew immediately that you are my Orla's twins, Kathleen and Gabrielle. I have prayed for this day. Could you indulge a silly old woman and give her a hug?'

For what seemed a long few minutes, the three held onto each other. They could feel Amelia's heart race in her frail body. Julie gave her a peck on the cheek while Caroline wiped a tear from her eye and patted her bony hand.

'My dears, we have so much to talk about, but first, Irish hospitality starts with a cuppa. You'll take a cuppa tae?'

'May we help,' said Caroline, as she followed her to the kitchen just off the hallway, accompanied by Julie.

'That will be grand, just grand.'

With everything ready, Caroline carried the tray to the sitting room where Amelia, with a shaking hand, poured tea and handed it around with homemade biscuits.

'These look delicious,' said Julie, as she placed one on her plate.

Then Amelia spoke. Wiping her eyes, she began, 'You have to excuse me. Sure, now, I'm never as emotional as I feel right now. So, where to begin? Firstly, which one of you is Kathleen?'

'I am,' smiled Julie. 'I believe I was born first.'

'Yes, my dear, you were. You came into the world without a fuss and were placed in my arms, while this one here,' she nodded towards Caroline with a smile, 'this one, Gabrielle, gave her sweet mother quite a time of it.'

They all laughed at the mental image Amelia had painted of their arrival into the world.

'I was always a trouble-maker,' replied Caroline.

Julie commented, 'We only met each other yesterday; neither one of us knew of the other's existence until recently.'

Amelia looked horrified, 'Begorrah, you mean you weren't adopted together? We understood the nuns had organised a couple to take both babies. God preserve us.'

'Nuns?' quizzed Caroline. 'Where do they come in our lives?'

'Oh, my dears, we have so much to talk about. Sure, now, let me start at the beginning, when I answered an advert for a governess/nanny to look after three children of the Coogan family. I had an interview and was given the job of looking after two lovely young boys and their beautiful sister. They were good children, just grand, and I had no problem with them. The boys were sent to boarding school to be educated by the priests, and I was left with seven-year-old Orla. To be sure, I was only ten or eleven years older than her and we became more like sisters. Her parents wanted her educated at home, and I became responsible for her all-round education.

'I was glad she hadn't been sent away like her brothers, who came home on holiday and wept in my arms as they told me the horrors they experienced at the hands of older boys. Sure, and weren't these others just hooligans, if you ask me. The boys pleaded with me to beg their father to let them stay at home and attend the local school, but sure, wasn't he the most stubborn man on God's earth. He refused and told them it would be the making of them.'

Amelia paused to draw breath, as if painful memories were resurfacing.

'Is it too much for you to go on?' asked Julie anxiously.

'No, my dear. God himself sent you to me when he put you on my doorstep. You have a right to know and I have a duty to tell. Anyway, time went on as time does. The boys finished school. Gerald the eldest went to Dublin University to study commerce, while Anthony took a degree in agriculture and farm management. He loved the land and was always pottering around the estate following Steve – a grand fella if ever there was one. You met him, a grand fella. Anthony was forever bending his ear on gardening matters. It was one summer when it happened, and the boys were at home.

'Orla turned into a stunning young colleen and, like most teenagers, had a mind of her own. Sure, and she had that. She would go off alone on long walks around the estate and refused to say where she had been. She wasn't normally troublesome, but she was at the age where she wanted her independence, free from the restraints of her father. Well, one day I found her weeping in her room. It took a while for her to confess that she had a boyfriend who told her he didn't want any more to do with her. Sure, now, and it took persuasion from her brothers to get her to reveal the name of the boyfriend, William Hanrahan – a local hooligan who worked on the estate. You can see where this story is leading, can't you?'

The girls nodded; they knew what was coming next.

'The inevitable happened. He had made the sweet inno-cent girl pregnant. Well, I tell you, all hell broke loose, with her father rampaging after him. The lout laughed in his face. The master collared him, threatened him with the Garda, and after getting some kind of apology from him, gave him a considerable sum of money on condition he tell no-one what had happened and leave the village immediately. Hanrahan was ecstatic. He never had money to spend, so promised he would move from the district as part of the deal and never reveal his source of cash or what he'd done to poor sweet Orla.

'However, that very same evening, he was drinking heavily in the local pub and boasting about another notch on the bedpost. Word got to Gerald and Anthony, and with a few friends they waylaid Hanrahan and gave him a beating. Hanrahan was never seen in the area again, but several months later his body was pulled from the sea. A post-mortem concluded that he must have fallen in when drunk, his bruises were consistent with a fall. Mysteriously, the exact amount of money that he had been given was deposited in Orla's bank account. The devil got his own.'

'And Orla?' questioned Caroline, 'What happened to her?'

Amelia shook her head. 'She was banished to Scotland, with me in charge of the poor girl. Had it not been for his religious beliefs, the master might have arranged for her to have an abortion. Thank the good Lord above for that, or you two colleens wouldn't be sitting here now. Ah well, where was I? Her father rented a small apartment where we set up home until it came time for her to give birth. My poor lass developed complications and it was feared she would miscarry, so she was taken to a maternity home run by nuns for the last few weeks of her pregnancy. It was a home for unmarried women and girls, and while clean and spotless, it lacked any love. In fact, she told me the nuns were quite rough with her, telling her she had the devil in her. The poor girl was bereft. They told her, they did, that she must have supped with the devil. Now, who would say that to a sweet, innocent girl? When I was allowed to visit, which wasn't often, she would weep in my arms and beg for it to be over. She was so frightened, my poor Orla, especially when they told her there were two babies. Sure, now, and she had only just turned seventeen.

'Anyway, on one of my visits, she went into labour and I was allowed by some sort of miracle to be with her during the birth. I think the nuns were hoping for a substantial monetary gift, knowing she came from the landed gentry, and wanted me to report how kind they had been to Orla. Her father had arranged for the babies to be adopted together. Orla, heartbroken in two, held you both for a short time; two days was all the time she had with you before they took you away. We were both hysterical, by God. I had to keep strong for her, but it wasn't easy, as I was churning up inside.

'After the birth, we went back to the apartment but neither of us could settle. She refused to return to Ireland – she was a much stronger woman by then, a grand woman she was turning into. So, we remained in Scotland and moved to another area to seek employment, she as a shop assistant and me as a part-time governess to a family who only required their son to have help after school. I think they wanted me to do his homework for him to get good grades, but I made him do it himself with my guidance and support. It was a job and, sure, it paid the bills.'

Amelia looked at the two engrossed faces and continued.

'Her parents never acknowledged that they had grand-children by Orla, telling everyone that she was teaching in Switzerland. After their death, she had a wish to return to

Ireland – God's own country, to be sure. Gerald, the eldest boy, had inherited the estate and welcomed us both with open arms. A grand lad, he was, just grand. We lived in the house for a short time, but neither of us was happy there. There were too many ghosts to lay, too many bad memories. Anthony had moved to New Zealand to help run a sheep farm. We never saw him again, although he keeps in touch and we enjoy the craic. He married late in life to a New Zealand woman, Tammy, much younger than him, and they have twin boys – identical boys, Samuel and Howell. So, it seems twins run in the family, isn't that a fact?

'Eventually, running the estate proved too much for Gerald; times were bad with recession that saw him lose the bulk of his investments. He had been given bad advice, but he was fortunate to sell the place at a reasonable price to a developer who had ideas to turn it into what you saw today – a gaudy hotel if ever I saw one. A grand house turned into a circus. Orla and I moved here to this little cottage and made it our home. Sadly, Gerald died of a heart attack, God rest his soul. It was so sudden; we were shocked at the speed of it.'

Julie asked tentatively, 'And Orla, when did she die?'

Amelia looked momentarily stunned. 'Oh, my dears, didn't you know? Sure, now, your mammy is still alive, did no-one tell you?'

∞

They looked at each other in total bewilderment.

Caroline whispered, 'Our birth mother is alive?'

Amelia nodded, wiped a tear from her eye, and continued, 'She's alive in body, but not in mind. She is in the late stages of Alzheimer's; it got her very young. I noticed her memory was not as sharp as it had been, and over the past few years she deteriorated quite rapidly. I nursed her here in the cottage, with help from carers, but it was becoming too much for me. So the decision was taken out of my hands when she had a fall and was admitted into a care home. It's only a few miles from here and I visit once a week. It's so upsetting, as she sometimes doesn't know me. And her only now reached her seventieth year; too young to be in that state of ill health. Sure, she has a lot of living to do, but who can question the ways of the good Lord who seems to know what's best for us? Not that He's asked my opinion. She lives in the past, poor lamb, and often mumbles what sounds like "my babies, my babies".'

All three were sobbing now, and Julie hugged the bereft woman and let her cry on her shoulder.

'Oh, what a silly billy I am. Forgive me, girls, it's been so emotional. I think we need another cuppa tae, and what about some supper? I have proper Irish hot pot ready. I must have known you were coming. Yes. I knew you would come. Begorrah, I knew you were coming.'

During supper in Amelia's cosy kitchen, and with the girls complimenting their host on her fine hotpot, more questions were asked and answered. When they'd finished, Julie mentioned that they were planning to drive on and find a guest house or hotel for the night. Their plans were flexible.

'Sure, I'll not have Orla's babies going off to a guest house. I have a grand twin-bedded room that you are welcome to have. It was actually Orla's room. When she became ill, I had her large bed exchanged for two beds so that I could be with her during the night. So, my darling girls, you may spend the night here in your mammy's room. I'll put the kybosh on any ideas you have of staying in a hotel, and you are as welcome as flowers in May to stay as long as you like.'

The women looked at each other then smiled at their host and announced that they would be honoured to stay there.

Amelia was not finished, though. 'Tomorrow, if you like,' she said, 'we will visit Orla. Yes, we will. We'll visit your mammy.'

∞

After Amelia had retired for the evening, the sisters talked well into the night, discussing everything they had heard about their origins. Julie questioned why their birth mother hadn't shown up on the DNA investigation.

'Maybe there's more to this story than we've been told,' replied a sleepy Caroline. 'Or Irish records may be different. Who knows? Do you want to visit her tomorrow?'

Julie lifted her head from the pillow and mumbled, 'We've come this far, let's see it out. Anyway, I'm anxious now to meet her. Let's get some sleep.'

'What a cosy room this is, and to think our mother slept here in this very room. I wonder which bed she slept in.'

There was no reply. Julie had fallen asleep.

Next morning after breakfast, Amelia took them on a tour of her garden. She was a keen gardener and enjoyed pointing out various plants and flowers. 'Of course, nowadays I depend on help from a young lad from the village who keeps things under control; a grand lad he is, too. Orla was never one for the garden. Weeds could grow around her feet and she wouldn't notice. She always had her nose stuck in a book. She had no interest whatever in gardening.'

Julie laughed, 'Just like me. I have the most neglected garden in the village. Every two years there's a competition for the best village in bloom, and the organisers despair when they view mine. They usually send a team in to tidy it and put me to shame.'

Caroline chuckled. 'I never had much interest in gardening, and living in an apartment doesn't actually help the situation.'

Amelia tut-tutted. 'Just like Orla. I did everything in my power to get her interested in gardening, but sure, nothing would entice her to pick up a spade.' Looking at Caroline and wagging her finger, she continued, 'Young lady, you could have a window box. There's no excuse.'

Julie could sense something of the love and care that Orla had received all her life from her nanny-governess and her best friend. Such a sweet lady, she was to tell Maggie and Liz later.

After morning coffee in the garden, Amelia announced she was going to call the care home to arrange a visit. 'I don't like to go too early, as the staff have a lot to be getting on with, God bless them. Afternoons suit them.'

'Isn't she a darling lady?' remarked Caroline, as their host went indoors to make the call. 'I think she has accepted us into her life and into her heart. She's the kind of mother I would have loved, to steer me along the right path and keep me out of trouble. I don't know about you, but I feel very comfortable with her.'

'Yes, I do, too,' Julie agreed. 'Orla was fortunate to have her in her life. She's so non-judgmental about Orla's indiscretion. Our poor mother, how hard it must have been to have her babies taken like that. I don't like the sound of her father, our grandfather, do you? Or our father, for that matter.'

Before Caroline could reply, Amelia came across the lawn, her face ashen, her shoulders slumped, and her pace slower.

'Oh, my dears. Orla has taken a turn for the worst and is

drifting in and out of consciousness. I fear she has not long for this world. Matron suggests if you want to see her, we should go now.' Amelia was distraught. 'I don't know what I'll do without her. I've prepared myself for this day, but now it's here... We best be going.'

She turned to the sisters and asked, 'That is, if you still want to see her.'

'We do,' they answered almost in unison.

Julie drove carefully, following Amelia's directions, and turned into a driveway where the care home sat in a neat, landscaped area.

They helped the distressed lady into the home where she was met by Matron who hugged her, took her arm, and whispered, 'It won't be long. I'm glad you came today. I'll leave you all with her and pop in later.' She smiled at the sisters and said, 'Amelia told me who you are. Orla constantly calls out for her babies.'

Amelia led them to a pretty room – bright, airy, and beautifully decorated. There in the bed lay the mother they had never known. Orla looked serene and calm, and the girls immediately noticed the resemblance to themselves.

Leaning nearer, Amelia whispered, 'Orla, darling, your babies are here to see you.' She motioned to Julie to sit by her birth mother. 'Just talk to her. She will hear you, but probably won't be able to respond.'

Julie sat by the bed, held her mother's hand in hers, and put her mouth near Orla's ear. 'Hello Mammy,' she whispered. 'It's Kathleen come to see you.' As she held her hand, she felt Orla grasp her finger, her eyes fluttered as she mumbled incoherently. Caroline changed places and following Julie's example whispered, 'Hello mammy. It's your Gabrielle here to see you.' She planted a kiss on her cheek and saw a tear drop from Orla's face. Once more her eyes flickered, and she grasped Caroline's hand.'

The girls sat together, each holding one of their mother's hands, and took it in turn to chat to her and reassure her they had a good life and had always wanted to find her; there was no point in saying anything negative. As they spoke, Orla appeared to pick at something on her nightdress, drawing their eyes to a pretty locket.

Amelia spoke to her. 'I'll show your babies what's in here, shall I?' She didn't expect a reply and unfastened the little locket, opening it to reveal two separate little compartments – each containing a tiny curl of hair and an initial beside each one: K. and G.

'Sure, now, and she's worn this every day of her life. It's all she had to remember you by. Before the nuns took you away, I cut a little bit of hair from each of you and later bought this little locket.'

Unwilling to cry in public, Caroline left the room to sob her eyes out. Julie, normally a strong, unemotional person wiped a tear from her eye then kissed her mother on the cheek and continued to sit by her side. Words weren't necessary.

Amelia pinned the locket back onto the nightdress, 'There you are darling, the locket is safe.'

Julie ran her long hair gently across Orla's face and down her arm. 'I have long hair now,' She whispered, and once more she felt Orla's hand twitch.

Matron had been watching from the door and entered the room, smiling as she told them, 'She is responding well, she knows you are here.'

Caroline returned, having composed herself, and took her birth mother's hand again. She had never expected to feel such an emotional reaction to anyone other than Blake.

The three sat with Orla for a few hours, each taking it in turn to calmly talk to her, sometimes sitting in silence holding her hand, or stroking her hair. There was an air of serene acceptance in the room. Matron popped in, offered tea and scones, and checked the patient.

'Her breathing is becoming more laboured,' she remarked.

Without warning, Orla opened her eyes, squeezed the hands of her children, smiled, and drew her last breath. It was a moment or two before they realised she had passed.

Amelia gasped, kissed Orla's cheek and whispered, 'Goodbye, my darling. Sleep with the angels.' She left the room with Matron who held her by the arm and helped her out to the garden.

∞

Back at the cottage and after the inevitable cup of tea, the girls let Amelia cry and talk about Orla for as long as she needed, while they comforted her as much as they could.

'I must contact Anthony. What time is it in New Zealand? Sure, and I can't get my head around the time difference.'

Having established that it was a suitable time to make contact, Amelia set up her computer and clicked on Skype. The sisters moved out of earshot to allow her the privacy she needed to give Anthony news of his sister's demise.

'Aw, Nanny,' he used the name he always called her. 'It wasn't unexpected, from what you've been telling me, but, aw, my little sister, gone to be with Gerald and the angels. I'm glad you were with her when she passed, that would be a comfort for you. God rest her soul.'

'Sure, and I wasn't alone with her. You will never believe it, but two real angels were with her.'

'Yes, Nanny,' he soothed, 'I know the angels come at the moment of death. That is consoling, too.'

'No, Anthony dear, real angels. Her babies, grown women now, who turned up at my house yesterday searching for information on their birth mother. Orla's Kathleen and Gabrielle were with their mother when she passed. She knew they were there, and it gave her great comfort. Would you like to say hello? They are right here in my sitting room.'

'Oh yes! This is nothing short of a miracle. Of course, I'd like to say hello to my nieces.'

Amelia signalled to the sisters to sit by her and be introduced to Anthony.

'Hello,' began Julie, 'I believe you must be our uncle. I was the first born, I'm Kathleen, and here beside me is Gabrielle.'

They looked into the smiling face of their newly-found relative – a refined gentleman, weather-beaten from years of outdoor work.

'This is amazing. You turned up in time to meet my dear sister at the right time,' he told them, with a hint of Irish brogue mixed with a Kiwi accent. 'She must have been waiting for you. She truly believed she would see you in this life. She constantly spoke of her babies. It was heart-breaking for her to give you up for adoption. She never really got over it, and I never forgave my father for sending her away. She could have stayed. Sure, it would have been a scandal for the Coogan family, but these things happen, and it would have passed as a seven-day wonder.'

They spoke at some length before leaving Amelia to finish her conversation and close down her computer. Sometime later, she joined them in the kitchen where Caroline, with Amelia's approval, made supper.

'Anthony wants me to postpone the funeral until he gets here,' she told them. 'He's off to make travel arrangements. I never thought he would want to make a long journey again, but he's determined to come over.' She frowned and looked thoughtful. 'I must contact the funeral directors to make arrangements. My dears, can you possibly remain for the funeral?'

Julie hugged her and replied, 'I've come all this way, and I'll be here for you. I just have to Skype my friends to let them know my plans.'

Caroline, still very emotional, nodded that she too would remain. 'I'll contact Blake and let him know. I'll ask if he'd contact my workplace to arrange for compassionate leave for me.'

During their stay with Amelia, the sisters learned more of their birth mother's life and her place in the Coogan family, and enjoyed the opportunity to get to know each other better. Their hostess produced a box of photographs that three heads pored over, with Amelia describing various people and events.

'Orla is so like us in this one,' remarked Julie, adjusting her reading glasses and sharing the picture with her sister.

'Yes, sure, you are like your mammy. As soon as I saw you at my door, I knew immediately who you were. God sent you to us at the right time. Anthony was right when he said Orla was waiting for you. God rest her dear soul.'

∞

With everything in place for the funeral, accommodation had been reserved at the local hotel for Anthony, who insisted his nieces remain with Nanny. He had made the arrangements himself and he had given Amelia a rough idea when he would arrive.

A car drew up at the gate and, minutes later, Anthony entered the cottage.

'Nanny, I'm here. Your favourite little boy.'

Amelia gave a squeal of delight as he scooped her into his arms. 'Oh, how happy I am that you've come to help lay Orla to rest.' Overcome with emotion, she snuggled into the strong arms of the man she had helped to rear, and wept until she had no more tears to shed. They stood there for the longest time until Amelia broke away. 'Come and meet your nieces.' She led him by the hand to the sitting room where the sisters were busy folding the Order of Service booklets.

'Anthony, meet your nieces, Orla's babies.'

They both stood to greet their newly-found uncle and were soon enveloped in his strong arms.

'I've longed for this day,' he told them. 'In my heart I knew you would be found. Oh, how like Orla you both are.'

'I'm going to put the kettle on,' announced Amelia. She was about to head to the kitchen when Anthony halted her.

'Nanny, there are some people I want you to meet first.' He went outside and signalled to the people sitting in the car to come into the cottage. 'Nanny, meet my lovely wife Tammy, and my sons, Sammy and Howell.'

Amelia squealed with delight and could hardly contain herself as she looked at the trio, who stood smiling but bemused as they spotted Julie and Caroline, who hovered in the background, not wanting to intrude on the family's privacy. Amelia had spoken to Tammy and the boys over the years by Skype, but she was overwhelmed to see them here in her house.

'We thought it would be a good opportunity for us all to meet, albeit in sad circumstance, but I'm sure dear Orla is looking down on this gathering with pride. We thought a surprise visit would cheer you up.'

Tammy, a few years younger than her husband, smiled as introductions were made. She was casually dressed, her long hair tied back, showing a firm jawline and an honest face.

'I had to come to meet the other set of family twins. Here are my two, can you tell the difference?' She laughed as she made the introductions. 'These two take great pleasure in confusing people. School was a nightmare, with teachers asking me to dress them differently, but they swapped clothes and made life extremely difficult. And as for getting them to admit to misdeeds, well, that was nigh impossible.'

The ice was broken as two handsome young men were drawn into the conversation. 'Hello there, I'm Sammy – older and wiser than this brother of mine. And don't believe all that my mother tells you about us. We are innocent until proven otherwise.'

His jovial nature lightened the sombre mood that had broken Amelia's heart.

Howell stepped forward to give Nanny, as they had always heard her referred to, a bear hug that had the elderly lady giggling until tears of laughter rolled down her face.

Eventually the kettle was put on to boil, and the group sat at Amelia's kitchen table discussing their life in New Zealand and enquiring about Julie and Caroline's lives. Anthony was annoyed to discover they had been grown up separately.

'I was under the impression that you were adopted together by a wealthy family. That was the arrangements made by my father with the nuns. If I had known you weren't together, I would have made enquiries, and I'm sure for all his gruffness, my father would have dealt with it, too. Deep down, he really wanted the best for you both, but he couldn't forgive his daughter.'

They spoke of Orla's first meeting with her daughters, with Amelia praising God for sending them to their mammy in her final hours. There wasn't a dry eye in the room; even the young men were caught up in the emotion of their aunt's death.

With details of the funeral to be discussed, Tammy declared she wanted to stretch her legs and explore the garden. Both sets of twins retired to the sitting room and compared likes and dislikes, the brothers telling tales of fun they'd had going through life confusing people.

'We had a bit of confusion, too, although we've only just met,' said Caroline, and she looked at Julie for approval. 'Shall we tell them about Edinburgh and Blake?'

Julie nodded her agreement and Caroline told the tale of Blake's experience.

It was a contented group that dispersed for the night, with Amelia ecstatic at having so many of Orla's family together.

∞

The day of the funeral began with a Spring drizzle that soon changed to warm sunshine, as the family gathered outside the little church of St. Mary's in the village. The church-yard was crowded, with mourners from all areas of Orla's life paying their respects to the well-loved lady. Steve, the gardener, was there with a beautiful wreath that he had fashioned himself. Matron and a few of the care home staff were also in attendance. Villagers of all ages lined the path to the church, then, to Julie's delight and shock, Maggie and Liz appeared at her side.

'We had to come to be with you as you laid your birth mother to rest,' whispered Maggie, as she hugged her aston-ished friend. Julie turned to look for Caroline to introduce them, and found her twin crying in the arms of a well-dressed, good-looking man.

'Yes, it's Blake,' stated Liz. 'We met him by chance on the plane, got talking, and discovered we were heading to the same funeral. And, of course, we recognised him from the Edinburgh encounter. He insisted on sharing the driving and cost of the hire car, but we got lost and arrived quite late last night at the village hotel, so decided not to call on you at such a late hour.'

Just then, the church bells that had been ringing one stroke for each year of Orla's life, stopped and the mourners headed into the little church. Anthony led the way, hand-in-hand with Amelia, Tammy walked behind them with her sons on either side of her. Julie and Caroline walked together and heard a few gasps from the congregation as they looked at two grown women who so closely resembled Orla.

Father O' Sheridan, who Amelia told them had faithfully attended to Orla's spiritual needs, welcomed everyone and remarked on how full the little church was.

'Your presence here today is a measure of your love and respect for a delightful lady.' He continued by welcoming the visitors, 'Orla's brother Anthony and his wife and sons travelled from New Zealand to pay their last respects, and to support Amelia who has been with the family since the children were young. I'm delighted to also welcome Orla's daughters, her twins, Kathleen and Gabriella, who were with their mother in her final hours. You are all very welcome.'

After the service, the mourners walked a short distance to the churchyard, where she was laid to rest beside her brother Gerald. The local hotel organised a meal for the mourners, giving everyone an opportunity to reminisce about Orla. Julie and Caroline found themselves objects of curiosity, as many locals were unaware of their mother's past.

Managing to extract themselves from curious villagers, Blake took Caroline by the arm and led her to a quiet spot where she wept tears for lost years with her birth mother and her twin; and for a life that could have been so different.

Julie, with Liz and Maggie by her side, walked to Amelia's garden to catch up with each other. 'You have no idea how much it means to me to have you both here,' she told them. 'Whose idea was it?'

'Maggie's,' replied Liz. 'After your last Skype session, we decided to fly over for you. Girl, you've been through a traumatic time and need your best buddies by your side.'

Julie told them about everything that had transpired since she set foot on the Emerald Isle, culminating in the death of her mother. 'It was a moving experience to meet her in such circumstances,' she admitted. 'Oh, how I regret not searching for her many years ago, but it is what it is.'

Maggie asked, 'What are your plans now? Will you fly home with us?'

'I've decided to stay on a bit. I don't want to abandon Amelia when she's so vulnerable, and I want to get to know Anthony and the family – my family.' She smiled. 'It sounds quite strange to call them that, but in a way, it is comforting. I never thought I would experience such an emotional rollercoaster. They are staying around for a little while, and Anthony has organised a tour of Harmony Meadows to show his family where he grew up. Would you like to join us and see my ancestral pad?' Julie giggled at the thought of having such a house to show off.

'Wouldn't miss it for the world,' replied Liz enthusiastically. 'We need to compare it to Maggie's little pad.'

Julie felt more loved than at any time before in her life. She had found relatives she never knew existed, and felt a new phase was about to begin in her life. She also felt drawn to explore her Irishness – the culture, the people, and her newly-found family. She had connected well with Amelia, the woman who had been present at her birth and who knew more about Orla than perhaps anyone else, and Julie was determined to keep in touch.

'I can envisage a few visits to Eire in the next few years,' she told her friends, as they sat together in Amelia's garden, relishing time together. The bond of friendship that had begun when they first met as schoolgirls, was as strong as ever. And they laughed as they recalled their visit to Edinburgh when Blake had unwittingly frightened them by his persistent calling out to Caroline.

'Poor guy. He must have thought you were some kind of madwoman who didn't recognise her own fiancé,' Liz giggled as she remembered the incident.

'And I thought he was a madman. Being accosted in an Edinburgh hotel is a scary prospect,' added Julie, 'and not one that I recommend.'

Maggie, the thoughtful one of the trio, asked, 'So, what now for Julie Sinclair? A change of name perhaps, now that you know your origin.'

She shook her head. 'No, no. I don't plan on changing my name. I'm Julie Sinclair and wouldn't feel comfortable as anyone else. Names define people, don't they? What I might do in future books is write as Julie K. Sinclair, but that's as far as name changes go.'

As they chatted, Blake and Caroline arrived hand-in-hand and joined them in the garden. 'We have some news for you,' said Blake with a smile. 'We held back after everyone had gone and spoke to the priest.' He turned to Caroline and said, 'Do you want to tell them?'

Caroline smiled, squeezed his hand, and said, 'We are going to be married, here in St. Mary's. Father O' Sheridan is arranging for paperwork to be in order and agrees it would be lovely for us to wed while Anthony and his family are staying in the area, touring around. As soon as we have a date, we hope they will come back to the village.'

Blake continued, 'We asked Father O' Sheridan if we were being disrespectful, having a wedding so soon after Orla's death, but he assured us we were good to go ahead and thought Orla would have wholeheartedly approved. We haven't told Amelia yet, but I'm sure she will be delighted. Julie, will you stay on? And Liz and Maggie, we would like you all to be with us.'

'We wouldn't miss it for the world,' replied Maggie, as she offered congratulations to the couple. 'We had intended to stay around as long as Julie needed us. There's no rush for us to head home, and I would love to explore a bit of Ireland. Galway is stunning.'

'That seems settled then,' remarked Julie, as she hugged them both. 'Of course, I'll be at my little sister's nuptials. And is a change of name on the cards for you, Caroline?'

Blake laughed, 'We've had the option of so many name changes over the past while, I'm beginning to get confused about my identity. I plan on ditching the Jessop name and taking my mother's name. So, Blake David Carter – at your service, ladies,' he added with a flourish of an imaginary hat.

'And I will be Mrs Caroline Gabrielle Carter,' announced his bride-to-be.

'Amelia will be delighted that we are going to include our birth names, although I think she will forever call us Kathleen and Gabrielle,' smiled the elder twin. 'Blake, what about your birth family?'

'I plan on talking to my mother this evening by Skype, and inviting her over. I'm not sure how that will be received, but we'll wait and see. It would be the icing on the cake if she were here with me. Isn't it surreal that we've been searching for our birth parents at the same time? Who would ever believe it?'

Caroline squeezed his hand in recognition that she understood how much it meant to him. 'We'd better go and find Amelia. I don't want her hearing the news second-hand. Julie, will you be my maid of honour and walk down the aisle with me?'

'I will be delighted, my dear.' She chuckled, 'I've only just found you, and now I'm to give you away.'

∞

Back in Yetts Bank, Liz's husband, Colin called in at the post office to send off some items to Liz. Not missing a trick, Jessica Morris remarked, 'A parcel to go to Ireland? Oh my, and to Galway. Is Liz on holiday? I must say I haven't seen her around for a few weeks. Or Julie for that matter. Are they off on another holiday?' She emphasised the word 'another'.

Colin, always looking for an opportunity to tease the inquisitive lady and feed her curiosity, replied, 'They're attending a wedding.'

'I love weddings. Who is being married?' Jessica was almost over the counter, ready it seemed to prevent Colin from leaving the shop before she had gleaned every detail from him.

'Julie's sister is being married in their family estate.'

Colin could hardly hide his smile as the woman gasped and almost begged for more.

'I didn't know Julie had a sister,' she retorted, quite offended at the omission. Her voice was raised an octave or two and Colin though she might become apoplectic if he didn't feed her more information.

'Oh yes, her identical twin. Didn't Julie mention her? That must have been an oversight on her part.'

'And there's a family estate?' questioned Jessica, removing her glasses to wipe them on her sleeve, as if in doing so, she would hear more. 'An identical twin?'

'Yes, a large estate, now an upmarket spa resort. The wedding reception is to be held in the grand ballroom. Well, Jessica, I must rush off now. I'm checking on Julie's house while she's away. Imagine you not knowing she came from the landed gentry.'

As he left the shop, he heard the stunned woman almost pleading for more. 'But... but... who... what...'

Colin chuckled to himself as he drove downhill to check Julie's premises. I shouldn't tease her like that, but I couldn't resist it.

It was not long before the entire village of Yetts Bank would know that Julie Sinclair came from Irish aristocracy and had an identical twin, while Jessica was left thinking, I wonder if she's been here and I've mistaken her for Julie... wonder what her name is? What Jessica didn't know, she made up.

∞

As Jessica pondered over the name of Julie's twin, the person in question was in the throes of changing her name. The wedding of Caroline and Blake was a happy affair. The bride, resplendent in a functional but stunning outfit, walked down the aisle with her twin sister by her side. Her groom was grinning from ear to ear as she approached the altar, where he stood with Anthony as his best man. The

Kiwi cousins were ushers and played their part well in leading the guests to their seats, but not before escorting Amelia to her place of honour at the front. Tammy sat with Liz and Maggie, and to Blake's delight, his mother had made the journey with Riley.

'Mum didn't need much persuasion to be here,' said Riley, 'she's been so excited.'

Father O' Sheridan had a twinkle in his eye at every wedding he conducted, as he attempted to put nervous brides and grooms at ease. As he welcomed the congregation, he looked at Julie, and announced, 'Sure, now, I hope I get this one right and match the groom to the right bride.'

The new Mr and Mrs Carter emerged into the sunshine to a round of applause. No official photographer was required, as everyone it seemed had a mobile camera. After they had all had clicked to their satisfaction, the bridal party drove the short distance to Harmony Meadow Spa Resort. Amelia was at first reluctant to revisit the family home, knowing memories would surface of the strict master and his treatment of Orla, but common sense won, and she joined the others.

Anthony, sensing her hesitation, led her by the arm into what had once been home to them both. The resort manager and staff had excelled themselves in decorating the ballroom to welcome to the family. After the meal, and with dancing in full swing, guests mingled and caught up with each other's news. Julie was particularly interested in chatting to Blake's mother and sister.

'It's been a whirlwind of emotions for us all these past months,' she remarked to the woman who bore a marked resemblance to Blake.

Riley, a confident, bubbly woman, chatted as if she had known Julie all her life. They shared life experiences and found they had a common interest in books.

'Riley seldom has a book out of her hands,' said her mother. 'Ever since babyhood she loved to have stories read to her. Blake tells me you are a writer. What do you write about?'

For the next hour, they discussed books until Blake arrived to take his mother for a slow foxtrot, leaving Riley to quiz Julie to her heart's content.

'Will you write about finding your mother?' she asked. 'That was eerie that you and Caroline were searching at the same time, not being aware of the other's existence. And Blake, too, searching for mum. It's all intertwined, isn't it? It's surreal.'

'Yes, smiled Julie, 'it must be a twin thing. They say twins have a special relationship, but we've missed out on that. We have a lot of catching up to do. As far as writing goes, I've actually begun to write a semi-autobiography. Whether or not I include Orla and Caroline, remains to be seen.'

'My mother was ecstatic at finding Blake. She had always longed for that day, but circumstances at home were difficult and she had to wait until our father passed away. As much as I loved my father, he was overly strict and would have made life unbearable. Everything has worked out well, though, and I have a new brother and sister-in-law.'

∞

Julie sat with Amelia on their last evening together. So much had happened in the past few months for the elderly lady to take in. Everyone had returned home with memories that would linger for many years. Julie had remained to ensure Amelia was content and coping without her beloved Orla.

'I really am fine, my dear. I am at peace knowing that she had her babies by her side, and for me to see one of you married off and having my dear Anthony here, has made me very happy indeed. You do not need to fret about me, I'll be fine, sure. After all, I have my garden to attend to, so you can go back home knowing you've made an old lady happy.'

'You won't get rid of me that easily,' smiled Julie. 'I plan to come back in a few months.'

'Sure now, and wouldn't that be grand. That would be grand indeed. Come for Christmas. I can't promise you a wild time, it may be too quiet for you, my dear, but it would be lovely to spend time together. Blake has promised to bring Gabrielle over early next year, so I'm a very contented old lady.'

'Lovely. Yes, let's do that, and as for wild times, I'm way past that stage in life.'

∞

Back home and with Jessica's curiosity satisfied, life for Julie at Yetts Bank continued as before, but with the added knowledge that life would never be quite the same. With her new-found sister and Anthony and Amelia keeping in regular touch, she now appreciated belonging to a family, surprising herself at her repressed feelings of ever wanting to know about her start in life. Her life with her adoptee parents would always be special, and they were and would remain her first family. She returned to her writing with new-found motivation to include her search for her life story in her autobiography. As Christmas approached, she made travel arrangements and returned to Galway.

∞

I take up the pen to continue my life story. So much has happened in the past year that both surprised and scared me, as events unfolded at a pace that saw my confidence in myself challenged to reveal suppressed emotions I had never allowed to surface. This strong woman, this Julie Sinclair, does not succumb to emotions. I was gently coerced into searching for my birth parents and, had it not been for my childhood friends, I would never have known the joy of meeting my identical twin – my Rebecca perhaps, from childhood. Our upbringing was dissimilar: mine, a happy contented one; hers, many miles metaphorically from my experience, was disturbing. I rejoice now in how her life has been turned around with marriage to her darling Blake.

Julie smiled as she looked at Amelia dozing contentedly by the fireside. Christmas for them had been a time of reflection, of tears, laughter, and sheer joy. She had made the journey to spend time with the woman who she had taken to her heart, and found herself calling her Nanny, much to the delight of the recipient.

'Amelia is getting on a bit,' she told Caroline, 'so I plan to spend as much time with her as possible.'

Looking around the cosy sitting room, filled with treasured pictures of Amelia's charges, Julie felt a connection with them all: with Orla, her mother; Anthony, her uncle, his wife and their amusing twins; and Caroline and Blake, whose wedding picture took a prominent place on the sideboard. Poignantly, she would never meet the man whose face shone like a light from the silver picture frame that Amelia kept nearby. But she would learn of her Uncle Gerald through family stories. She sighed with contentment as she closed down her laptop.

Amelia had suggested she write her book in the quietness of the cottage.

'After all, sure I'm likely to doze off to sleep and leave you quite alone. Indulge my old age quirkiness.'

The only sound was the gentle ticking of the clock and, to Julie's amusement, the occasional purring from the sleeping lady. Julie stretched her arms, tousled her long hair, and sat contentedly on the comfy sofa, letting the warmth from the log fire fill her with a serenity she had not experienced in a long time.

During her stay, and with Amelia's blessing, she had taken long, winter walks, but the absence of her dogs felt strange. Liz had Skyped her on Christmas Day and showed the pooches dressed in Santa hats and tinsel.

'Looks like they are having fun and not missing me in the least,' she laughed, as she shared the pictures with Amelia.

On one of her walks just outside the village, she fell into step with another walker and his lurcher pup. They wished each other Happy Christmas as Julie patted the dog.

'She seems to like you. She doesn't usually take to people. She's a rescue dog and very timid. Her name is Speed, a nod to her breed. Do you like dogs?' enquired the stranger.

'I do indeed. I have two at home in Scotland and miss them when I go for walks. I'm so used to them being by my side.'

As they spoke, the man said, 'I'm Declan by the way. Declan Walsh, and you must be Amelia's guest.'

This was Ireland, where everyone knew everyone else, and visitors were treated as family. Irish hospitality was renowned worldwide and Julie had certainly experienced it on the few occasions she had visited.

'Yes. Pleased to meet you. I'm Julie.' They shook hands and walked together for a bit, chatting mostly about dogs.

They parted company at the church and Julie went to her mother's grave to offer a quick prayer before heading back to the cottage. Not being a religious person, she had discovered something of the value and consolations that faith had brought to the people she had met recently, especially Amelia, whose cottage was full of religious icons that brought the old lady comfort.

For her remaining time in Galway, Julie took several walks, explored different paths, and relished the freedom to roam. My thinking time for writing, was how she described it to Amelia, who was happy that her Kathleen was enjoying the area.

Occasionally, Julie would meet Declan and Speed, and walk with them. She found the amiable Irishman easy to talk to, and shared some of her life story with him as if she had always known him. She gently prompted the reserved man to do likewise and, once he engaged in conversation, he relaxed in her company. He looked forward to bumping into the interesting woman whose presence in the village with her sister at the time of Orla's death had caused much craic among the inhabitants.

Julie, too, looked forward to walking with him, and instead of leaving meeting to chance, they began arranging a time and place to begin their walk.

They found they had much in common. He loved reading and hiking and the outdoor life, and of course, dogs. His height matched hers, and his dark brown hair had a tendency to fall over his hazel eyes that seemed to sparkle as he smiled.

Julie secretly admitted to herself that she looked forward to seeing him. But nothing escaped the sharp eyes of her hostess.

'Wasn't that yourself now that I saw at the gate with that fellow Declan Walsh? And him a clever lawyer with a posh house in Dublin?'

'Oh, Amelia, you are incorrigible. You know fine well it was Declan. We've been going for long walks and he's been showing me around the area. We get on well and he's asked me to a ceilidh on Friday night.'

'To be sure, and him a credit to his mammy. The poor woman did a grand job of bringing him up after his daddy died in a train accident when the babby was only about two-year-old. A grand woman is Maeve Walsh. Sure, now, wasn't it her that got him through the university by taking every job she could to pay for his education. A grand woman, the best mother-in-law that any colleen would be proud to have.'

Julie threw her head back in raucous laughter, tears of hilarity rolled down her cheeks. 'Amelia, you are way ahead of yourself. Declan has asked me to a ceilidh to show me a bit of Irish culture. It's a dance, not a marriage proposal.'

'Sure, and don't two people shorten the road. You would do well to think about his motives. Now, isn't he the best of son to his mammy, a grand woman is Maeve Walsh and him a clever lawyer in Dublin. Mind you, it would take a special woman to take him from his mammy. Sure, and aren't Irish men the ones with a bond to their mammy that can never be broken.'

'We only go for walks together, and he loves dogs, too, just like me. We have a lot to talk about.'

'And didn't the good Lord above make all the creatures. Many a creature has brought a couple together. Now, don't you go thinking he'll be a grand dancer. Sure, aren't Irish lads the worse dancers on God's earth, unless the name is Michael Flatley. You go ahead and have a grand time. That's what it will be, a grand time.'

Julie retired for the night, laughing quietly at Amelia's matchmaking wiles. Wait until I tell Maggie and Liz.

∞

Julie's plan to return to Yetts Bank did not go as planned. On hearing her travel plans, Declan suggested they travel together as far as Dublin and spend a few days there together.

'Ah, it would be grand to show you Dublin town before you head home.'

He proved to be an informative guide, and enjoyed watching her reaction as they walked around the city, pointing out places of interest.

'I never knew that Dublin was so beautiful,' she said as they sat by the River Liffey enjoying people watching and laughing together as they shared more of their life stories. They visited St. Patrick's Cathedral where Julie, in awe of the interior, followed Declan as he pointed out the magnificent stained-glass windows, the enormous pillars and arches, and gave her a brief history of the building.

'I'm in awe of this place, it takes my breath away. But is it always so busy, so noisy?'

'The down side of this beautiful building is that so many tourists come to see it. Sure, the cathedral depends on their donations to keep it going, but the noise takes something from the sacredness of the place, don't you think?'

Julie caught something of the spirituality of the quiet, gentle man she felt at ease with. Declan stopped at the burial site of Jonathan Swift. 'You being a grand writer will know who this is.'

'Ah, yes, the satirist, the author of Gulliver's Travels,' gasped Julie, as she donned her reading glasses to read the inscription. 'Not one of my favourite poets, but it is good to see he has been honoured here.'

They left the cathedral and headed to Phoenix Park and Dublin Zoo, where the animal lover in her spent a few hours admiring the various residents. They each snapped pictures of the exotic Chilean flamingos and watched them for some time.

'There's so much more to see in this city that you'll have to come back and stay for longer,' remarked Declan as he asked permission to take her picture. 'A memento of your first Dublin visit.'

A passer-by stopped and spoke to them. 'Now wouldn't it be just grand for you two lovely people to have a picture taken together, just to capture the love between you.'

Julie, slightly flustered, handed over her camera phone, saying, 'Oh, we're not...'

She didn't get any further as Declan, directed by the photographer, moved in closer and put his arm around her. The moment was captured.

∞

Life for Caroline, with Blake by her side, saw her more secure and contented than she had ever experienced. They visited Blake's family as often as possible, much to Lisa's delight, as she got to spend time with her David. The couple moved to a new house to be near Lisa and, to Caroline's delight, Blake arrived home one day with a puppy.

'He's a rescue dog, a bit of everything. They say mongrels make good pets, so here you are, your own little pup that I promised to get for you once we were settled in our own home and had a garden for the little fellow to run around in.'

Caroline was elated as she held the sleeping pup in her arms. The past few months was a frenzy of activity and fun as they decorated what was an old house that had not seen a paintbrush for many years. Caroline had a good colour sense and carefully matched wall decorations with textiles. They looked forward to many years together in their dream home with Toots – as she chose to call her pup – the centre of attention.

Caroline was keen to keep in contact with Amelia, the person who was there for her during birth and marriage. Having Orla's girls in her life helped the elderly lady cope with her the loss.

As the trio sat around enjoying the craic, Blake turned to his wife and whispered, 'Will we tell Amelia our news?' She nodded in agreement.

'Nanny,' he began, using the name they were all comfortable with, 'We have some exciting news. Anthony has invited us to New Zealand for an extended stay. We've been keeping in touch with him and the family and were thrilled when he suggested we visit. Of course, we accepted. I always promised Caroline that I'd take her on travel adventures, so this is perfect for us. We'll be gone for three months.'

'Sure now, isn't that the best news ever. It will be grand, just grand.'

Caroline continued the conversation. 'We wanted to visit you before we fly out. Our only problem is Toots here.' The pup in question who had travelled with the couple, picked up his ears on hearing his name. 'However, everything is working out fine as Julie has agreed to have Toots join her brood of dogs. One more dog to Julie will be no trouble at all, so it seems.'

'So,' said an excited Blake, 'when we leave here, we're heading for Yetts Bank to deposit Toots and to see Julie's little village. Neither of us have been there, we're so looking forward to the visit.'

'Now that will be grand for you all to be together. Kathleen wanted me to go back with her last time she was here, but, sure and aren't I getting a bit long in the tooth for travel. You young folk make the most of life, for the years fly past in a flash, as I know.'

∞

The whirlwind time in Dublin with Declan ended too quickly for Julie who returned home with emotions in turmoil, mixed feelings that kept her awake and disturbed her sleep. There was nothing else for it, she had to contact her best buddies and listen to their words of wisdom. Liz had arranged to call in to return the dogs to their owner and Julie took the opportunity to have a girly chat with her. After a welcome-home hug, and pats for the exuberant dogs, Liz remarked,

'You seem different girl. Has something happened to you over there in your Irish home? I observe a glow about you. Am I to drag it out of you? There's a serenity about you that wasn't there before.'

Julie, instead of speaking, reached for her camera, passed it to Liz, and waited.

Liz gasped. 'Julie Sinclair, tell all, right this minute. Who is this gorgeous hunk?'

'His name is Declan Walsh, he is a partner in a law firm in Dublin, and happened to be home for Christmas to be with his mother who lives a stone's throw from Amelia. We met by chance while I was out walking, and we got talking.'

'And?' questioned Liz grinning at Julie's discomfort. 'Girl, get Skype set up. Mags needs to be in on this.'

Fumbling with her laptop, she eventually connected with Maggie who was relaxing at home. Liz wasted no time in starting the conversation, 'Hi there, Mags, just look what our Julie has been up to when our back was turned. Come on, girl, send the picture.' Maggie donned her glasses, clicked on 'full screen' and let out a cry of delight.

'Right then, tell all. He's a honey.'

Liz, the instigator of the conversation, related all she knew to their friend.

'She's only gone and bagged herself a handsome, Irish lawyer with a house in Dublin where, listen to this, our Julie stayed for three nights... now, what's your take on that?' Liz laughed at Maggie's expression.

'Well, my dear, as I heard dear Amelia say, What's for you won't go by you. My, he is a looker.'

Eventually, Julie with tears of laughter running down her face, managed to butt into the conversation. 'You two are incorrigible, you're talking about me as if I wasn't here and, for the record, we had separate bedrooms.'

'I believe you,' laughed Maggie, 'but I'm not sure others will. When are we going to meet him?'

'You two are as bad as Amelia. She had me married off after only one walk with him in the snow. We met by chance...'

She never finished the sentence as both her friends roared with laughter, 'Okay, so you say.'

The conversation was light-hearted and fun, with Julie feeling the love and friendship that had followed her all her life from her two caring friends.

'Actually, he is coming to Yetts Bank soon, as are Caroline and Blake who are bringing their new pup to live with my brood while they traipse off to New Zealand to spend time with Anthony. They all want to see Yetts Bank. Maggie, you may as well invite yourself. I know you are itching to meet him, and Liz will no doubt be on the doorstep. I don't suppose there's any point in me telling you we are simply friends who enjoy each other's company.'

Liz and Maggie looked at each other on the screen, laughed, and shook their heads.

∞

Yetts Bank was buzzing with curiosity, instigated by Jessica Morris as she related what she called inside information to everyone who entered the hallowed door of her premises.

'You know I never gossip, but... wait until you hear this. Julie was in here yesterday, standing on that very spot, and purchased provisions the like of which she never did before. Julie, I said, are you having visitors? Yes, she told me. I am. My sister and her husband and another friend are coming at the weekend. Oh, I said, would that be your twin? Jessica, yes, it is, and you'll get to meet her, she said. There you have it, straight from the horse's mouth. Well, I was so taken aback that I omitted to ask who the other friend was. I wonder who it is. Maybe another famous writer like herself.'

Jessica let her mind wander and her imagination took over, and before long she had embellished the story of her conversation with Julie. So much so, that she couldn't quite remember the original details.

Julie drove to Edinburgh to meet Declan and took him on an Edinburgh tour bus to show him a quick tour of the capital. 'This is the best way of seeing Edinburgh, or any city when you have only a short time; it gives a flavour of the place.' They sat close together on the top deck totally at ease with each other.

As they passed a hotel Julie said, 'Here's the hotel I told you about where Blake approached me, thinking I was his Caroline. We laugh at it now, but at the time it was terrifying.'

With the tour over and Declan heaping praise on the city he had always longed to visit, they drove home to Yetts

Bank. Their arrival did not go unnoticed, as Jessica knew the sound of Julie's rather old car and popped her head out of the door as it passed the post office. Julie waved, smiled, and drove on.

Well, if I'm not mistaken, there's a man sitting in the passenger seat. Well, well.

If only Jessica had an excuse to knock on Julie's door on the pretext of delivering stamps or some products, she would have been there before the car was parked.

∞

It was Jonny, Maggie's practical husband, who first broached the idea for a joint birthday celebration.

'You gals have been close since childhood, so why not celebrate together, the three of you? And of course, there's Julie's twin. It's a great opportunity while Declan is here.'

'Jonny, you have surpassed yourself. What a brilliant idea. I'll contact the others and talk it over with them.'

They agreed to hold the event in the Edinburgh hotel known to them. Julie volunteered to contact the manager whom she knew, to discuss the possibility of holding the birthday dinner there.

'My dear Ms Sinclair, it will be a delight to welcome you and your party. I'll transfer your call to Stefan our events manager to discuss your requirements.'

Once arrangements were made, Julie contacted Caroline and Blake to ask them to extend their visit to Yetts Bank for the dinner party.

'Blake, it will be held in the hotel well known to us both,' she told him. 'We've arranged for overnight accommodation there before we all head back to Yetts Bank.'

They laughed together as they recalled the embarrassing incident.

Maggie had been staying with Colin and Liz while Declan was with Julie, who had introduced the affable Irishman to the eager postmistress.

'Let's get this over with,' she laughed, as she warned him what to expect from Jessica and her probing, unrelentless questioning. As it was, Jessica was almost dumbstruck as the handsome gentleman took her hand and kissed it, saying how wonderful it was to meet her, and that he had heard so much about her from his friend Julie.

He excused himself stating that he was expecting an important call from his business partner and regretted not having longer to chat. Julie could hardly contain her mirth as they drove to Safe Haven for the eagerly awaited introduction to her inquisitive friends.

Jessica had enough information to impart to her customers for several days, if not weeks. 'Such a gentleman, they don't make them like that any longer, so polite, too. And handsome,' she added, as she studied her hand.

Surrounded by dogs of all shapes and sizes, the couple made their way to the house where raucous laughter could be heard.

'Anyone at home?' enquired Julie, and she led Declan to the sitting room where Liz and Maggie were engrossed in watching a film.

'Hello.' Liz almost screamed as she fumbled for the remote to silence the film. She stood to welcome them, giving Maggie, who was still wondering what happened to the sound quality, a gentle nudge to focus on who had arrived.

'Oh,' Maggie ventured as she noticed the others. 'Sorry, I was engrossed in this old movie.'

'Liz, Maggie, this is Declan, my friend.' She emphasised the word friend, not that either woman took any notice of it.

'Declan, these are the crazy friends I told you about. I love them dearly, but don't believe a word that comes from their mouths.'

After firm handshakes and tentative hugs, the four settled to talk. Julie sat back and smiled inwardly as her friends elicited as much information as they could from Declan without being too forward. With a wink from Liz, it was obvious that they had given the seal of approval to the good-looking Irishman.

Maggie had news for them all. 'Jonny insists on paying for our birthday bash as he can't be there in person to help us celebrate. He's been in touch with the hotel to finalise arrangements. You know what he's like, when he makes his mind up, no-one can change it.'

'How kind and typical of the man,' replied Liz.

∞

The birthday dinner was a huge success with Stefan and staff providing an exquisite meal. Geoff, the manager, insisted on providing wine for the table, and after desserts four members of staff presented each birthday girl with an exotic bouquet of flowers.

'These were delivered earlier today with instructions to be given out after the meal. Happy birthday,' said Claudia, as one by one she read out the names: 'Liz, Caroline, Maggie, and last but not least, Julie.'

The recipients of the flowers were delighted as they read the gift card and looked in surprise at the sender. Declan smiled in acknowledgment of their thanks and, much to his embarrassment, was soon smothered in hugs.

Julie whispered in his ear as she planted a kiss on his cheek, 'Thank you, you are the kindest man in the world.'

The moment was caught on camera.

∞

Once more, I take up the pen to continue my autobiography with a new spring in my step. Two years have passed since the joint birthday celebration. I am at a crossroads in my life and admit to being happier now than I ever remember. I am with the man I love. Life has moved on for us all. Caroline and Blake's decision to move permanently to New Zealand, after their successful trip to visit Anthony, was not unexpected as they enthused about N.Z. and the opportunities that awaited them. Their final visit to Galway to see Amelia was difficult for them as a strong bond had developed over the years. After all, if things had been different, my twin and I would have been brought up by Nanny Amelia. Toots now remains a permanent member of my doggy clan. As for my two good friends, Maggie is a doting grandmother to Robin and Amy-Lee's son, John-Edward, and is becoming a frequent transatlantic flyer, while Jonny is considering taking early retirement to spend more time with his family. Liz and Colin are still living nearby and have extended their premises and built up their business to include more pet services, with Malcolm having a permanent role as a business partner.

My visits to Galway are more frequent now, as Amelia is getting on in age and stubbornly refuses to slow down. With Maeve, Declan's mother, popping in on a regular basis, the two established a firm friendship, with their love of gardening at the centre of their shared interest.

My autobiography will perhaps be added to in the coming years, but for now, I end it with a dedication. To Orla, my mother.

Julie saved her work, closed down her laptop, and sighed with contentment as she looked at Declan who was quietly reading a book with three dogs at his feet and Speed on his lap. He looked up, put the book down, and said, 'Finished, darling? Time to open a bottle to celebrate.'

THE END

ABOUT THE AUTHOR

Terry H. Watson qualified in D.C.E. and Dip.Sp.Ed. from Notre Dame College, Glasgow and Bearsden, and obtained a B.A. degree from Open University Scotland.

A retired special needs teacher, Terry began writing in 2014, and to date has published ten books.

Terry welcomes reviews for her books.

You can contact her at:

Twitter: https://twitter.com/terryhwatson1

E-MAIL: terryhwatson@yahoo.co.uk

Website: http://terryhwatson.com

Facebook: https://m.facebook.com

Lightning Source UK Ltd.
Milton Keynes UK
UKHW040837301120
374359UK00001B/112